THE INVISIBLE KID
AND DR. POOF'S MAGIC SOAP

By Terry and Wayne Baltz

Red Feather Books

The Invisible Kid Series:

#1 *The Invisible Kid And Dr. Poof's Magic Soap*

#2 *The Invisible Kid And The Killer Cat*

#3 *The Invisible Kid And The Intergalactic RV*

Threshold Books

Night Of The Falling Stars

To Madeleine,

THE INVISIBLE KID
AND DR. POOF'S MAGIC SOAP

Terry Baltz

by

Terry and Wayne Baltz

Wayne Baltz

Cover Design & Illustration by Gary Raham

A Red Feather Book

PRAIRIE DIVIDE PRODUCTIONS
Red Feather Lakes, Colorado

This is a work of fiction. The characters, incidents, and dialogues in this book are all products of the authors' rampant imaginations and are not to be construed as real. Except, of course, while you are reading the story. And unless possibly all of this really did happen and no one told them about it.

ISBN 1-884610-11-0

For

Julie, Derek, David
and
invisible kids everywhere

⇌ One ⇌

I always wanted to be invisible. But I never expected it to *really* happen.

When I was little I used to prowl around the house pretending to be the One And Only Invisible Detective. I could see everybody and nobody could see me. That was better than even Sherlock Holmes.

But when I invisibly detected my sister, Penny, kissing her boyfriend behind the oak tree in our back yard, she didn't call me Sherlock Holmes. She called me "The Little Snoop."

And when I invisibly detected my mom wrapping a big box before my birthday she said, "Cassandra Ann, don't you have something to do?"

And when I got up one time in the middle of the night and invisibly detected my dad in the kitchen making a sandwich he said, "Hi, Casey. Want some peanut butter?"

But all that was before I got mixed up with Dr. Poof and my friend Kathleen's weird Uncle Terence O'Toole. That's when I really did get invisible.

And that's when all the trouble began.

* * *

It was the last day of fifth grade. Kathleen and I go to different schools in St. Louis County. She's in private, I'm in public. But both our schools let out the same day that year and I rushed over to her house so we could celebrate our freedom together. I burst in the front door without knocking and yelled, "Kathleen!" Nobody answered and I thought nobody was home.

Tap, tap, tap. That was a familiar sound. The basement door was open and I could hear Uncle Terence hammering away down there. Probably working on shoes again. He was always working on shoes, especially since he quit his job at the university. I tiptoed down the stairs to surprise him. But half way down I froze. Sweat beaded on my forehead.

I saw an odd-looking shoe in some kind of vise on Uncle Terence's workbench. A row of tiny nailheads stuck out of the sole. And above it, swinging in a graceful arc, a small hammer drove the nails in one by one.

Only nobody was swinging the hammer. Not Uncle Terence, not anybody. The room was empty.

I dashed up the stairs, my heart pounding through my chest, tripped on the top step and landed hard in the doorway. After checking for broken bones I wondered if my imagination had gotten the better of me. That's what my dad always says: "Your imagination's getting the better of you." When I was little he was saying it at least twice a week when I scrambled downstairs after seeing a ghost in my closet. He would walk me back up to my room and patiently search through my closet and under my bed without finding any ghosts. Then he would scruffle my hair and say, "Feel better?" And I would say, "Yes." Only I didn't feel better, because what does it really prove if you can't find a ghost?

As soon as the blood stopped jackhammering in my head I called out, "Uncle Terence?" No answer. I forced myself back down the stairs, stopping on every step, scrunching way down to see what I could before going further. All the way to the bottom.

There was nobody. Nothing. The shoe was in the vise, the hammer lay on the table. Like a hammer should when no one's around. I edged toward it, holding my breath and moving slower than a fish in mud. Then, with a lightning-fast move I grabbed it right behind the head, like it was a snake, pinning it to the table top. It didn't squirm or try to get away.

After about a minute of high-pressure pinning I began to feel a little silly. And my fingers started to cramp. I picked the hammer up with two hands, still keeping a tight grip. But the hammer-snake was dead. I *had* been letting my imagination get the better of me.

I put the tool back on the workbench and crept up the stairs, wondering the whole time what the hammer was doing now, and trying hard not to look behind me. I jumped inside my skin to see Kathleen in the hall.

"Hi, Casey. Have you seen Uncle Terence?" she said.

"No. It wasn't Uncle Terence."

"What do you mean? Who wasn't Uncle Terence?"

"I saw . . . I mean, I thought I saw . . . I mean I thought I *heard* him downstairs. But when I went down I didn't see anything. Nothing." She looked at me suspiciously. "Honest," I said.

"Casey, you're acting weird. What's going on?"

"I told you. Nothing." Kathleen tapped her foot impatiently. "Okay," I said, "so maybe I was just letting my imagination get the better of me a little bit."

"Oh. So what else is new?" She pulled two softball gloves out of the hall closet. "I swear, Casey, I don't know who is more strange, Uncle Terence or you."

Kathleen's Uncle Terence has always been unusual but since last fall when he quit his job he's taken to just vanishing at times. Kathleen and her parents can't find him in his bedroom or in his basement workroom. Sometimes he shows up in an hour. Sometimes in a day or two. Once he was gone for over a month. When Kathleen asked him about it he said he'd gone home. Kathleen said *this* was his home. Which was true: he and her father grew up in that house. He didn't argue but he didn't tell her any more, either. Just that he'd had to go. And that he was sorry for worrying her. Pretty soon he was back to his usual routine, making shoes. Lots of shoes. I don't know what he does with them.

Kathleen slapped one of the gloves against my stomach. "Let's play some ball," she said. "We've got our outfield back."

"The trailer's gone again?"

"Yep." We headed around the corner for the vacant lot.

We use it for choose-up games. It really belongs to the county, which hasn't had the money to make a park out of it. They rented the space to a small circus company last October, and when it left a couple of the carnival hands stayed behind with their trailer. I've never seen them but the trailer comes and goes and we never know for sure when the outfield's going to be clear.

Kathleen pounded the ball in the pocket of her glove. "I hope we can round up enough kids."

A lot of times it's hard to get a game going since most of the kids in the neighborhood like to watch television after school. I would never choose TV over a good ball game.

It's not that I don't watch TV. I do, but mostly only after midnight, when the really good movies are on. Like *Revenge of the Mud People* last night. My family doesn't know I do this late night watching because I set the alarm clock in my mind to wake me up at a certain time. Mind alarm clocks are an important detective tool because they don't make any sound. Then I sneak down to the kitchen and pull the portable TV under the table with me. I only do it once in a while, otherwise I'd get too tired and people would begin to wonder why. And too many people asking questions isn't good for a detective.

Anyway, I *was* tired after watching *Mud People*. I felt more like taking a nap than playing ball, but it was the last day of school and I wanted to celebrate. To my surprise, a lot of kids showed up and it looked like we'd be able to get a good game going. Mr. Bumps was there, too, waiting for me. He does that a lot — showing up where I am even though he didn't go there with me. Sometimes I think he can read my mind.

His full name is Mr. Harold T. Bumps and he appeared at our door about seven months ago. I remember because it was Halloween night. Cold, with snowy rain. I had just returned with my loot. "Here I am!" I announced, expecting a great "hurrah" or something. My dad grunted, Penny left the room dramatically, and my mom pulled my ghost sheet from where it was caught in the door. "How did you ever get this so dirty?" she wailed, as though it were a family heirloom.

That's when we heard the *bump*. It wasn't a knock. It was definitely a bump. I opened the door. A blast of freezing air poured in but that was it. I was closing the door against the bitter wind when a small black and white terrier dog walked right in. He shook himself from nose to tail and plopped down on the rug as if he'd always lived here. I named him that very night: Mr. Harold T. Bumps. I liked the sound of it. Mr. Bumps for short. Bumps for shorter.

Bumps sat on the sidelines watching the game. Kathleen played left, I covered center, and Jay Randolph was right fielder. Nobody's much of a hitter. Sometimes we stand out there the whole game with nothing to do.

"What's your uncle up to these days?" I shouted over to Kathleen while waiting for another Babe Ruth to come up to bat.

She shrugged. "Same old thing. Puttering in the basement."

"But what was he doing today, for example?"

"How should I know? I go to school, too, remember?"

Sometimes Kathleen gets exasperated at Uncle Terence and doesn't want to talk about him. She gets very disgusted with his disappearances and with his habits of smoking a pipe and drinking a "wee too much" as he likes to describe it. "But darlin'," I heard him tell her once, "I need my pipe to think. I need my whiskey to dream." She said, "I think, I dream, without the help of either." And she tapped her foot. She always does that when she's getting mad. "You're right, Kathleen, darlin'," he answered lightly. But there was a sadness in his eyes as he returned to the basement. I never understood why he gave in so easily since Kathleen isn't really much of a dreamer. On the other hand, I certainly am, and I don't need either, either.

I was considering what to tell Kathleen about the strange goings on in her basement when nosey Eddie Maskit came up to bat. What a pest he'd been all year. *Ball one.* If he wasn't asking the teacher stupid questions, he was pestering me. Following me around on the playground — *strike one* — and asking me a lot of personal things. "You look tired," he'd say. "What did you do, watch *Revenge of the Mud People* last night?"

Once he actually made me late for school — *strike two* — asking me all kinds of nosey questions about where Bumps came from and why he was named that and what the "T." stood for. He just went on and on and I wouldn't tell him anything and then, to spite him, I refused to get off the bus. *Ball two.* So did he. Then the driver got mad at us because we wouldn't get off and finally he left for his junior high route and I had to sit there with eighth and ninth graders *and* Eddie, which was the absolute worst hour of my life. I could live without him around. Believe me. Maybe I could feed him to the Mud People.

I was thinking about how much I hate Eddie when he hit a long, high fly out to center. The ball shot over my head like a rocket and I took out after it, knowing I didn't have a chance and that Eddie would be razzing me about his homer for the rest of my life.

Then a weird thing happened. Just before the ball landed it seemed to reverse course, and when it hit the ground it rolled right toward me. It was like it hit a wall or something. Only there wasn't any wall, or anything. Just clover, wild onions, and butterflies.

"Get the ball! Get the ball!" Kathleen and Jay yelled, rushing toward me from either side like crazed lunatics. I grabbed the ball, and shot it back to the infield. Eddie was out at third.

*   *   *

After the game I hung around and, when everyone else had gone home, I went back out to center field. Bumps came, too. I stood where I was when the fly ball went overhead. From there I slowly worked my way deeper into the outfield.

But not slowly enough. *Bam*! I grabbed at the sudden, burning pain in my knee. Bumps barked ferociously. There was something in front of us. Something very large and solid.

Something invisible.

⇌ Two ⇌

"What do you mean, the trailer's on the lot but it's invisible?" Kathleen demanded the next day when I told her what had happened. She tapped her foot and sent the porch swing into a nervous wobble.

"Just what I said. The ball bounced off it. Don't tell me you didn't see that!"

"The wind was blowing a gale out of center field," she insisted, tapping and turning the swing into a carnival ride. "Or there was a spin on the ball, probably." She huffed the way grown-ups do when they can't imagine something because it isn't right in front of them. Grown-ups miss out on a lot of good stuff that way. "Your imagination's getting the better of you again," she said, putting on twenty years in the space of a single sentence. I was getting mad. I mean, your best friend should believe you.

"I'm getting mad," I said. "Your best friend should believe you."

"But it's ridiculous. An invisible trailer. Anyway, what are you complaining about? He was out at third." She jumped off the seat and stormed into the house.

"Yeah, well that doesn't make my knee feel any better, does it?" I grumbled as I put the brakes on the swing.

Uncle Terence was sitting on a slatted chair at the far end of the porch. The odd thing was that I didn't see him before. I thought Kathleen and I were alone.

Like I said, he's Kathleen's uncle, not mine. But I've known him since I was little and everybody calls him Uncle Terence and he told me I should, too. Which I was glad of, because I don't even have an uncle.

He has red hair, mostly. It's turning gray around the edges, though, and he's a little bald. Which is easy for me to see because I'm the same height as he is, even though I'm eleven and only the fifth tallest girl in my class, and I guess he is at least forty-five or even fifty. Mostly it's his legs that are short. So short that, sitting there in the chair, his feet didn't touch the floor. His shoes, as usual, were strange. They were black, and square in the front, and each one had a large silver buckle on the top. I guess he made them himself because I've certainly never seen shoes like that in any store.

I've always liked Uncle Terence but he was scaring me now, just sitting there, nodding his head at me. And the pointy tips of his ears seemed to accuse me with each dip of his head.

I decided to take the offensive. "Do you know about the invisible trailer?" I asked. He raised his head and looked at me but didn't say anything. "What's going on around here?" I said. "Yesterday in the basement I saw your hammer moving in mid air without anybody holding it. Then nosey Eddie's fly ball is stopped by an invisible trailer. And now you suddenly appear on the porch out of nowhere." By then I was on my feet and kind of jumping up and down. In an agitated state, my sister would say.

Uncle Terence stood up and came over to me, his eyebrows scrunched together on his worried face. He put his hand on my shoulder in a fatherly way, a short fatherly way, and looked right at me. "If you hide from others, you only hide from yourself," he said. He said it very softly, as if he were speaking to himself. I waited for more but he just seemed lost in thought. After a while his eyes glazed over and I wasn't even sure he knew I was there.

"Thank you," I said, not knowing what else to do.

We shook hands. Uncle Terence always shakes my hand when we part, but he held on longer this time and his eyes, black and piercing again, told me to please give up whatever it was I was up to. Maybe I should have listened.

Instead, I raced back to the lot. I was surprised to find that it wasn't vacant anymore. The trailer was back. Or was it visible again?

I walked up to the trailer and around and around to the side away from the street, looking for clues. I found two signs, one on each side of the door. One said:

DR. POOF'S MAGIC TONIC
Makes Your Ills Disappear
Enjoy Perfect Health and Tranquility
Free Introductory Sample

And on the other side:

FORTUNES
Told By
Madame Helena Farsight
Adept in Palm Reading
and
Crystal Ball Gazing
Free Introductory Session

Magic tonic? Fortunes? Icy tingles cascaded down my spine. This was weird — better than any late, late superthriller on TV! Something was going on and Dr. Poof and Madame Farsight were definitely in the thick of it since it was their trailer that was playing peek-a-boo. But to figure it all out I would have to be clever. And careful.

I formed my plan right then. I would go in and ask for a free sample of magic tonic and a fortune and, when they weren't looking, snoop around all I could. Ask a lot of carefully worded trick questions, like detectives do, so nobody knows what I'm really after. It seemed like a sure-fire plan. Maybe a little short on details, but great detectives have to think on their feet.

I knocked, ready for anything.

⇌ Three ⇋

The door eased open. And it squeaked, just like in the movies. When the gap was no more than a foot wide Bumps came dashing around the corner of the trailer, scampered up the steps, and disappeared inside.

The door was closing. I squeezed in after him.

It was like walking into a darkened theater from a bright, sunny day. When I could see again, the show began.

Bumps was in the arms of a tall, thin, dark-haired man who wore an outfit like I've only seen at the circus. His pajama-like pants were purple, red, and orange and his shirt was bright blue. But he didn't have a clown face on.

"Welcome," he said, petting Bumps and staring at me from beneath caterpillar eyebrows. Like *I* was the strange one!

A woman came from the other end of the trailer. She was short and a little plump. She wore a full skirt of splashy bright colors, a red blouse, and a purple ribbon around her short, curly, jet-black hair. "I thought I heard a bump" — the man's nod toward me stopped her — "Oh. Company?" She sounded both surprised and pleased. "Well, come in, child. Sit down. Take a load off." She indicated a chair at a large round table that filled up most of the room. "What can we help you with today?"

"First of all I want my dog back," I said, thinking on my feet while Bumps wagged his tail and licked the man's chin.

Bumps is a friendly dog. He sleeps in my bed most nights and watches movies with me under the table and he follows me everywhere. But I've never seen him so friendly with anyone else. It bothered me.

"Give the little one her dog, dearest." She pointed from Bumps to me with fingers capped by inch-long red finger nails. "You must forgive us, child. This is the great Doctor Poof. He has powers even with a little dog he's never seen before. No harm was meant." The great Doctor Poof held Bumps out to me and I took him. Bumps looked back at Dr. Poof and fluttered his tail. Under a spell, I decided, and held him close. "My name is Helena. You can call me Madame Farsight. And I will call you 'little one.' All right, little one? All right."

She didn't give me a chance to get a word in edgewise. A word like "No!" for example.

"Now let me look into the crystal ball for you. You sit right here." She pushed me into a plastic and metal chair. "And I'll sit over there, all right? Ready?"

My mouth was hanging open. I didn't seem to be thinking too well anymore, on my feet or off them. She leaned over me very close as she talked and she smelled bitter, like burning leaves.

Finally, she shut up and sat down across the table from me. I held on to Mr. Bumps. Madame Farsight was in slow motion now, waving her hand over the crystal ball, repeating, as if to herself, "Monkey see, monkey do. Monkey see, monkey do." That's what it sounded like to me. "Monkey see, monkey do." I almost laughed, but she wasn't laughing. Her eyes got all glassy and she sat perfectly still. Her breathing got slower and deeper.

"Remember the tortoise and the hare," she said. Her voice was high and warbly, not like her own at all. There was a long silence. Oh yeah, I remembered, the tortoise wins the race when everyone expects the hare to win.

"No," Madame Farsight said sharply, in the strange new voice. Had I said something? I didn't think so. "The tortoise wants to know about the hare and about all others and about all things," she warbled. "But she does not want to be known herself. She hides inside her shell and thinks she is invisible. But the hare sees her anyway, and knows her better than if she did not hide. In the end, only she who hides is fooled."

She sat up straight and looked right at me, her eyes focused and back to normal. "Well, little one, that's it. That's my free introductory. How did you like it?" It was her usual voice. I tried to mumble something polite so I could get out of there fast, but my tongue wouldn't work. "What did I say?" she asked. "I never remember afterwards, you know."

A little kid, about two or three years old, lumbered out of the back room. Madame Farsight got up, ran to him, scooped him into her arms and said, "Madame Farsight will play with you in a minute, Kevin."

Kevin had blue eyes, blond hair, and wore totally normal clothes. He didn't look anything like his parents.

15

And Kevin didn't even sound like the name of a child belonging to Dr. Poof and Madame Farsight. A child of theirs should be called Merlin or Zodiac.

"I should take him outside for a while," Dr. Poof said.

"No, you can't take him out yet," she said quickly, moving away from the door with him. To me she said, "His skin is fair. He burns easily."

Who does she think she's fooling? Does she think I've never heard of kidnaping? Does she think she's dealing with an amateur here? I started inching my way toward the door. But Dr. Poof was there, holding a bottle and a small paper cup.

"Want to try some magic tonic?" he asked and pushed the cup toward me.

Oh, no you don't. I'm not taking any sleeping potion so you can kidnap me, too, I shouted inside my head. But Dr. Poof stood there, cup in hand, blocking my escape.

"I have to use the bathroom," I said, backing away from the table into a chair and almost falling over the couch. "Excuse me," I mumbled to the furniture. I held Bumps even tighter to my chest, ran down the hall, into the bathroom, closed the door and locked it.

It was a cramped room and I saw at once there was no window. Bad luck. I couldn't stay in there all day. And there was no way out except the way I came in.

I searched the shower. For what? A weapon? Incriminating evidence? Nothing there but a bottle of shampoo and a half-used bar of soap. Underwear hung on a line suspended above the tiny tub. The medicine cabinet had the usual stuff and it hardly seemed worth looking in the cabinet under the miniature wash bowl. But I was wrong. Something was there: a little box, high up in the back, almost out of sight, and taped to the wall. Hidden, I'd call it.

I reached in and carefully removed the tape. It was a little box, midnight-blue, with stars all over it. I opened it.

Inside was just a bar of soap. Not like the one in the shower, though, or like any I'd ever seen. It was cut into a rough rectangle and didn't have any picture or company name stamped into it. Following detective intuition I slid it back into the box and slipped the box into my pocket to check out later. Then I plotted my escape.

Brute force and blinding speed seemed like a good plan. I burst out of the bathroom, prepared to pulverize anybody between me and the outside door. But nobody tried to stop me. In fact, Dr. Poof was nowhere in sight and Madame Farsight just watched as I flashed by. Bumps whined a little as I jerked open the door and jumped the three steps to the ground in a single leap. Then I ran home faster than I've ever run before. Faster than when I was little and the ghosts were after me. Faster even than in track with Eddie Maskit coming up on my heels with his sweaty armpits and stinky breath.

For a second I thought I *saw* Eddie on the sidewalk near home plate but when I looked again there was nobody. I roared by without stopping to check.

* * *

17

I spent a very uneventful evening hiding my excitement from my family. It isn't too hard: nobody at my house ever expects anything interesting to happen anyway, so they tend not to notice when it does. I decided to shower and go to bed early.

I couldn't resist using the new soap. It smelled a little strange, like leaves burning in the fall. Like Madame Farsight, in fact. I felt bad about stealing the soap and made up my mind to return it as soon as I got the chance, and the courage to go back.

And I had to go back. I hadn't found out anything I'd gone there to find out.

I got into bed thinking I was probably exaggerating everything. Babies don't always look like their parents. Maybe he was adopted. And Kevin is a perfectly good name. Why couldn't Madame Farsight and Dr. Poof have named their baby Kevin?

Invisible trailer! I had to admit, it was a little hard to believe. Maybe I'd even apologize to Kathleen. I drifted off to sleep, pretty much convinced I'd let my imagination get the better of me.

But that was before I woke up to discover that sometime during the night I had disappeared.

⇌ **Four** ⇋

It was early and the windows were just getting some light. I swung one leg over the side of the bed. And screamed. There wasn't any foot sticking out of the bottom of my pajamas. I threw off the sheet and looked at the other leg. No foot there either. Little squeaky sounds slipped out of my mouth as I raised my arms to rub my eyes awake. Empty pajama sleeves hung in the air in front of me.

I fell out of bed in a panic. Ow! I did have hands and they were plenty sore from breaking my fall. I reached to where my feet should be. Something there *felt* like feet even if I couldn't see them. I stood up, wobbled like I do on the balance log at the playground, and fell down again.

"Casey?" My mother's voice registered somewhere in the back of my brain.

I got myself up once more and scooted across the floor like a first-time skater. In the full-length mirror on the wall I saw a pair of empty pajamas, upright and jerking along about three inches above the floor. No feet. No hands. No head!

I inched my way over to the mirror and extended a trembling invisible finger toward the glass. Touching it, I snapped my wrist back, as though I'd burned my finger on a hot stove. After a few more practice touches

I was all over the mirror with both hands. A trail of smudges followed my sleeve cuffs across the glass.

The mirror felt the same as usual. So did my hands. I just couldn't see them. I leaned forward and exhaled. A tiny mist clouded the glass, then disappeared. I looked inside my pajamas: all I could see were washing instructions and the floor.

I was invisible.

"Casey, are you all right?" Mom again, closer. I had to answer.

"I'm okay, Mom. Just fell out of bed." That seemed better than, "Help, help, I'm invisible!" Let's face it, sometimes honesty is not the best policy.

There was a *bump* at my door. Mr. Bumps, probably. I peered through the gap along the bottom to make sure. Dog feet. I opened the door a little and Bumps waggled through. Once inside though, he stopped abruptly, sat down, and whined. I closed the door.

"It's all right, Bumps." He shuddered and a nervous yip popped out like a hiccup. "It's all right." I reached to pet him and he jumped back, growling at my sleeve.

"Bumps, it's me," I whispered. "Come here. C'mon, boy. It's just me." His ears stood up straight and so did the hair on his neck. He came to me, but he resisted each step, sniffing the air for danger. I put my hand under his nose. He licked it and finally let me stroke him. His hair and ears relaxed and he sort of leaned into my hand. But he still whined like he didn't like it one bit. I petted him and petted him.

*　*　*

Knock. Knock.

I jolted awake from a wild dream that I was invisible. Bumps lay against my leg, asleep. I reached to scratch his ear. No hand. It wasn't a dream.

Knock. Knock. "Casey, are you there?" Mom's voice.

"Maybe she's still asleep." Kathleen.

"She was up an hour ago. Said she fell out of bed. Casey?"

There was a note of worry in her voice and I knew she would come in. Better they see nothing than this, I thought, and threw off the pajamas. They landed in a limp pile and the mirror showed that I was — gone!

In they came. I held my breath. Mom marched right toward me but I sidestepped to my desk. The only thing is, I knocked into my chair. It was only a little noise but enough to make Kathleen jump a foot.

"What was that?" she said.

"That's strange. I guess she's gone out," Mom said. "What was what?"

"That noise."

"Oh, Mr. Bumps I guess," she said absently as she picked up my pajamas. Kathleen stared at Bumps, who was sitting like a statue. I could tell she was suspicious, but she kept quiet. Good old Kathleen.

"I'm sure she hasn't gone far," Mom said.

"May I wait for her here?" She's my pal.

"I guess so. She probably won't be long. She hasn't had any breakfast yet."

"Thanks, Mrs. Granger."

21

I thought my mom would leave then but she didn't. She just stood there, looking around the room. She does things like that once in a while but I didn't like that she was doing it right now. She stared in my direction for what seemed like forever.

"What's that?" she said, pointing at me. My heart stopped.

"What?" Kathleen asked.

"There in the corner," she said, pointing harder. I couldn't breathe.

"Looks like Casey's" — it's all over, I thought — "softball glove," Kathleen said.

"Oh. Good. I thought it was a pile of greasy rags or something." I twisted around, careful not to make a sound. There behind me was my glove. She'd seen it right through me. Oh boy, this was getting better and better. "I guess I'm a little nervous about what she gets into," Mom continued, "after that fire with the chemistry set last winter."

"She said it was just a little fire," Kathleen defended.

My mother smiled the Grown-Up smile. "I'm sure she did, dear. They just seem so much bigger when they're right there in your kitchen."

"Yes, ma'am." Kathleen's very polite. She also knows when to fold 'em.

"I'll send Casey up if I see her," Mom said on her way out.

"Thanks, Mrs. Granger."

Mom's footsteps faded as she descended the stairs. "Close the door," I whispered. Kathleen obediently closed the door. Then she jumped a foot again. That girl ought to go out for the high jump.

"Casey?" she said.

"At your service."

"Casey? Where are you?" She looked quickly around the room, then under the bed.

"I'm not hiding, Kathleen. I'm right here."

"Stop playing tricks." She rushed around the room, looking behind the curtains and in the closet. I was having a little fun, I must admit. She even looked in a couple of dresser drawers, which made me giggle. She didn't like that a bit.

"Just stand still and I'll come to you," I said.

"Okay, but I wish you'd stop playing around. You almost got me into trouble with your mom."

"Here I am," I said, standing right in front of her.

"Where?" Her voice shook.

"Shh. Here, put out your hand." She put out one timid hand and I touched the tip of her finger. Like ET. Her mouth opened and her eyes got big and I thought she was going to scream, so I hit her on the back. Hard, like we do to stop each other from laughing to death.

She gulped. "What are you doing?" she whispered. "I can't see you."

"That's the idea," I boasted. I didn't hit her, but she yelped as if I had, turned completely around, and stared past me helplessly into empty space.

"I'm here. Right in front of you," I said. "Really."

"Casey, are you . . . are you . . . are you —"

"I think so," I said.

"Invisible?" The word was barely audible.

"Yes," I announced triumphantly, "as a matter of fact or fiction, I am." But Kathleen wasn't celebrating. In fact, it looked as if she might cry. I sat her down on the bed, which nearly made her faint instead.

"Was it the chemistry set again?" she whispered.

"The trash man's kids have the chemistry set," I reminded her.

"How did it happen then?"

"I don't know." I told her all about yesterday's weird events: getting inside the trailer, Dr. Poof, Madame Farsight and the strange fortune, Kevin, the hidden soap.

The soap. It could be the soap that made me invisible. The thought struck me as though the bar itself had been dropped on my head. A soap that makes you invisible. That was stupendous. I was the first invisible kid. And, I still *had* the soap.

"The soap," I gasped.

"Soap?" Kathleen said.

"I left it in the bathroom," I said. Where anyone might use it. I could just see Penny, or is it *not* see her, invisible. Could one invisible person see another invisible person? I didn't know. But either way, she wouldn't take it as good-naturedly as I did. Checking first to see that the coast was clear I tiptoed to the bathroom. The soap was still sitting there, next to our usual bar. I slid it back into its box and carried it to my room.

"This takes some getting used to," Kathleen said, watching the soap float into the room. "So what's the big deal about soap?" She was trying to sound nonchalant.

"Well," I said, "Dr. Poof advertises magic tonic. But if my hunch is right, this is Dr. Poof's magic *soap*. It's how I got invisible. I think."

"Who's Dr. Poof?" Kathleen looked sick. "Never mind. I don't think I want to hear any more," she said. "I'm going home now." No congratulations. No pat on the invisible back. Where were her manners?

"You can't go, Kathleen. Look at me." She tried. "I'm invisible. I need your help," I protested.

"And how long do you plan to be invisible?"

That was a scary question. It wasn't like I *had* a plan. But I wasn't going to let her know that. "Oh, for . . . a while." I casually tossed the soap into the air to show how cool I was about it all. Too bad I missed the box on the way down. "I don't exactly know how it works," I said, scuffling on all fours toward the soap.

"Not *exactly*?" she mocked. Where was her politeness when I needed it?

"No, not exactly," I persisted, as though the knowledge might come to me at any moment. "I took a shower with it last night. Then I got into bed and fell asleep. When I woke up I found myself . . . missing." I laughed, a little nervously. "Why don't you try it and we could find out how it works together?"

"No you don't," Kathleen said. "One of us has to stay normal, and you're out of the running. Besides, the point isn't to get me *in*visible but to get you visible again."

"Kathleen, how can you talk like that? I just got invisible. I want to try it out for a while. Just think of all the fun things I can do."

"But your mom's looking for you."

"Yeah, and she thinks you're waiting for me and that's where you can help out," I said. My mind was really clicking. "Go stand over by the window."

"What?"

"Just stand by the window," I insisted. She did. "Come outside, Kathleen," I said.

"What? You just said —"

"See? Now you can tell my mom you were by the window and I told you to come outside. When you go out I can sneak out with you. Pretty good, huh?"

"Do you know what you are? You're devious," she said. I waited. I know Kathleen really well. "Who's Dr. Poof?" she asked.

*   *   *

Going down the stairs, I tried to step in the same rhythm as Kathleen. I had a little trouble at first. I guess that was because I couldn't see where my feet were. Try it next time you're invisible.

At the bottom Kathleen went to the kitchen to talk to my mom. I was supposed to wait but I slipped quietly out the screen door. This is going to be easy, I thought. I can spy on people and they'll never even know I'm there. It couldn't be simpler! My foot slipped on the top step.

"Yaaghh!" I yelled as I pitched forward into space.

⇌ Five ⇌

Fortunately, I made a soft landing. Unfortunately, it was in the mushiest mud puddle I've ever met, face-to-mud.

What is my mother going to say when she sees me? I thought as I watched glop ooze between my toes. Then I realized that she wasn't *going* to see me. I was invisible.

I slipped and slid to my feet and looked down at myself. She might not see *me*, but she sure would see the mud plastered to my skin. I looked like I'd been attacked by the Mud People. Or become one of them.

I was standing there, feeling and looking ridiculous, when Kathleen and Mr. Bumps came out the front door. Bumps barked. Kathleen squished up her face in her usual pre-scream way.

"Don't you scream or I'll splash you," I said.

"Oh, it's you. I thought I ran into a chocolate-splattered ghost." She snickered.

"Ha, ha. Very funny." I pretended I was going to splash her anyway. She only seemed semi-scared, though. Maybe because she could only semi-see me. "Just go and get me some paper towels or something, would you?"

"Paper towels? You look like you need a car wash."

I put my hands on my hips and scowled at her the way Mom does when she's had enough of me. That didn't seem to work, either. Luckily, I happen to know that Kathleen hates to get dirty. I came at her, mucky fingers outstretched. That had the desired effect. She ran up the steps like she was being chased by King Kong.

"What'll I tell your mother?" she said.

"Use your imagination, Kathleen. And hurry."

She disappeared inside.

I was alone. And muddy. Alone and muddy and naked. And very visible. I snatched glances far and near, left and right, at yards and windows and porches, hoping the nosey neighbors weren't watching. What I saw was Eddie Maskit popping wheelies down the street. What was nosey Eddie doing hanging around on my block? I dove into the clump of snowball bushes beside the steps. Branches poked and scratched at me. Bumps sniffed and snorted, then settled down next to me.

The screen door banged and I heard Kathleen saying, "Your mom wasn't in the kitchen so I brought this, too." I peeked out. She had some dish towels over her shoulder and was lugging a bucket full of water down the steps. At the bottom she did a slow, wobbly spin. "Where are you?" she said. It wasn't a friendly question.

"Shh. Over here. In the bushes." Eddie seemed to be gone.

"Don't do that," Kathleen said.

"Don't do what?"

"Hide on me like that."

"I'm not hiding on you. I'm hiding on Eddie Maskit and other nosey people. Why didn't you bring paper towels, like I said?"

"These are more ecological."

"They're also our dish towels. Anyway, I don't care about ecological. I'm invisible. I care about hiding the evidence. That's what's important now."

"Ecological is always important. Being invisible doesn't change anything," she said. She seemed to enjoy pouring the water over my head.

"Did you ever hear of warm water?" I said.

I shivered and rubbed myself warm again with the towels. Even though the mud was washed off I wanted a shower. We decided her house would be safer than mine. We walked along, Bumps following at what he figured was a safe distance, barking all the way. Kathleen didn't like it since it looked like Bumps was barking at her. "Bumps, be quiet," she snapped, turning and wagging a finger at him. "Uh, oh," she said.

"What?"

"Casey, look what you're leaving behind you," she said.

"Oh my liver," I whispered. Muddy footprints followed us down the sidewalk. I hadn't cleaned the bottoms of my feet. It looked like Kathleen, who was wearing shoes, was leaving barefoot prints. Being invisible was a complicated business.

I rubbed my feet in the grass. We watched two parallel strips of grass bend flat and streak with mud. No footprints anymore, though. Bumps even stopped barking, but he still kept his distance.

We didn't see anyone as we snuck up to Kathleen's room. I showered in her bathroom. When I came out I was glad to find that she had lunch spread out on the bed. Apples, cheese, crackers, and peanut butter. Yum.

I sat on the bed and reached for some cheese. "I'm starving," I said.

"Don't do that," Kathleen said.

"Haven't we been through this once before? Don't do what?"

"I don't know. It just makes me nervous, not being able to see you." She grabbed her red cotton robe from the closet and handed it to me. "Here. Wear this." I put it on and tied the sash.

"Better?" I asked.

Bumps growled. Kathleen stared. Then she laughed, and cracker crumbs sprayed out of her mouth. "I don't know if it's better or not. Look at yourself."

"I don't have to. I look like the headless horseman, in a red robe. Right?" I began to eat again. I could still feel Kathleen's eyes on me. "Now what?" I said.

"Excuse me, Casey," she huffed, "but it happens to be just a little strange, watching a piece of cheese rise off the bed and then —"

"Well, try to live with it, okay? I'm hungry."

While we ate I told Kathleen my plan. "I can't go home like this and I don't know when I'll be visible again. That means I have to stay overnight at your house," I said.

"That's a great plan," Kathleen said. "My mom and dad love invisible kids."

30

"Of course they don't," I said, ignoring her sarcasm. "That's why we won't tell them I'm here. We'll just tell *my* mom." Kathleen tapped her foot. "Okay, okay. *I'll* tell my mom."

I called home. "Mom, can I stay at Kathleen's tonight?"

"If her parents don't mind," she said.

"They won't mind," I said. "They won't even know I'm here."

"See you tomorrow, then," she said. Maybe, maybe not, I thought.

Then I told Kathleen the second part of my plan. Well, not all of it. "Let's go on over to the lot and see if the trailer is still visible," I said. Kathleen agreed, although she called it going to see if the trailer was "there." I took off her robe and threw it on the bed. Kathleen started to complain at me, but before she got two words out Mr. Bumps jumped up and walked around and around on it, the way dogs do, making a nest. He lay down and wouldn't get up to come with us.

The trailer was there, plain as the nose on most people's faces. I wanted to get inside again, to find out if Dr. Poof and Madame Farsight had discovered their soap was gone and also to see if I could find out who Kevin's real parents were so I could tell them where he was.

We walked up to the door. "What are we doing?" Kathleen said.

"Ask for a free introductory fortune," I said.

"I'm not going in there. No way," she said. I expected that. I knocked good and hard on the door.

Madame Farsight answered so fast it was as if she'd been waiting on the other side of the door. I gave Kathleen a little push.

She said, "Uhhh." That's all the encouragement Madame F needed.

"Hello, little one. Glad to see you. Come in. Come," she said. An arm swathed in rainbow colors flashed toward Kathleen. The woman took my friend's hand and she was whisked inside, like a fly on a frog's tongue.

I followed, a shadow in the night.

⇌ Six ⇋

"Sit down over here and I'll tell your fortune."
Kathleen didn't move. "Right over here. Come. Sit."

Madame Farsight pushed down on Kathleen's
shoulders. She sat, stiff and straight in the chair, a
stunned expression on her face. She didn't say a word.
While Madame Farsight went into her trance I hurried
to the back part of the trailer. I tried to move without a
sound but that old trailer squeaked whenever it had a
mind to. I knew Madame Farsight wouldn't notice while
she was in the trance but I worried about who else
might be in the place.

The bathroom was empty. There was only one
bedroom. I peeked in the open door. A bed, a desk, a
chest of drawers, and a baby bed crowded the little
room. Kevin was the only one in the room and he was
sleeping soundly.

He looked so innocent and helpless. I wondered who
his real parents were and how I could help him get
home to them. Madame F's trance voice gave me the
courage to slip into the room. A second later I was
rummaging in the desk for incriminating evidence.

And in the second drawer, I found it. A lot of
documents, one of which was a birth certificate for
Kevin Spelling, born to Dr. Paul and Dr. Helen Spelling

at St. Louis Children's Hospital. That proved it. Dr. Poof and Madame Farsight were not his parents.

The front door squawked. "Come again, child," I heard Madame F say. I threw the documents back in the drawer, flew down the short hall and out the door with Kathleen.

"Casey?" Kathleen whispered when the door had closed behind us.

"Right here," I answered.

"What did you do that for?" Her words crackled like sparks from a fire. "I didn't know what to say or anything."

"What *did* you say?" I asked.

"Nothing. She said everything. She called me 'dear one' and 'child.' How revolting. And she said" — Kathleen imitated Madame F's high-pitched, zombie-like trance voice — "'watch out for the tortoise, she can get you into trouble.'" Then in her normal voice Kathleen said, "Isn't that weird?"

"Yeah." Weirder than she knew. Did Madame F talk about tortoises to everybody? "Did she mention the missing soap?" I asked.

"No. Why would she? I didn't take it." Her face fell. "Oh, no. You don't think she knows I know you, do you?"

"Like that would be the worst thing that could happen to you, huh?"

"Well you're the one sneaking around her house taking things," she said. "Anyway, did you get in or what? Did you find anything?"

I gave her a dirty look but, as usual, it did no good. "I'm giving you a dirty look," I said.

"Why?"

"Because, you call me a sneak and a stealer and then you want to know what I found out."

"Oh."

We walked, neither of us saying anything. Oh well, I decided, I can't wait around all day for an apology. "I found his birth certificate," I said. "Kevin's. His parents' name is Spelling."

We raced to her house and looked in the phone book. There was no Paul or Helen Spelling listed in the St. Louis area. I couldn't believe it. Kevin was only about two or three. Had his parents just given up? Maybe not, I decided. But the alternative was just as bad: maybe Kevin and his parents lived someplace else. Carnivals travel all over the country. The Spellings could be anywhere. My heart sank.

"Dinner in three minutes, Katie," her mother sang from the kitchen.

"Okay, Mom. Be right there," Kathleen sang back even though I happen to know she hates the name Katie.

Kathleen promised to bring me some food but when she returned with only a piece of bread and a pear stuffed in her pocket — "We had chili," she said — I was disappointed. More important, I was starving again. I'm always starving.

After everybody was asleep I crept down the stairs to raid the refrigerator. As I passed the basement door I heard Uncle Terence, humming something sad. I lay down on my stomach and peered down the stairs. He was just sitting there in his rocker, not doing anything. Just smoking his pipe and drinking something that looked like water, but I knew wasn't. It made me realize how often he had that melancholy, lonely look in his eyes. He's hiding something, I thought, some part of himself that I've never seen. I wanted to go down, just to say hello. But I couldn't. I was invisible.

I was lying there, feeling sorry for myself and Uncle Terence too, when he stood up and walked right toward the rear wall of the shop. He was walking fast, like there was an open door in front of him instead of solid concrete. Then something strange happened, and I mean very strange. Instead of smashing into the wall he seemed to go right into it. A golden glow outlined and erased his advancing body wherever it met the wall's surface.

It only took a moment. Uncle Terence was gone.

⇌ **Seven** ⇌

I rushed down the stairs. My invisible heels skidded over the edges of the last six steps and I hung on to the banister for dear life.

At the back wall, where Uncle Terence had disappeared, I pushed and pounded and slapped the cold concrete with my open hands. It was as solid as it looked.

Still, I had seen what I had seen: Uncle Terence, a golden light, then half of Uncle Terence, then none of Uncle Terence. My eyes, or my imagination, told me he'd walked right through the wall! I'd expected to find a fake spot, an interlocking Star Trek door or something. I pushed and punched some more. Hoping at least for a loose block or a secret passage. Anything.

But there was nothing. I decided it was time to just set myself right down in Uncle Terence's chair and wait for his return. I'd have to watch carefully, too, because the last time I saw what I saw, I almost didn't. So I fixed my eyes on the place in the wall where he disappeared. I stared until the skin on the backs of my legs got sweaty and stuck to the seat of his rocker. I stared and stared and stared for the longest time. Detective work can be pretty boring when you're on a stakeout. . . .

When I woke up, Uncle Terence was tiptoeing up the stairs. I tiptoed after him but all he did was go into his room and close the door. I felt like kicking myself for missing everything.

I was cold and hungry and tired of being a detective. I ran to Kathleen's room and dove into the empty twin bed. Good thing he didn't sit in his chair anyway, I thought, pulling the blankets over my head.

* * *

The next morning I was as invisible as ever. What if I stay invisible today? Mom expects me home to do chores.

That was a horrible thought, no matter how I looked at it, so I put it right out of my mind. Besides, there were plenty of other things that needed thinking about: Uncle Terence and the wall, the kidnapers, Kevin and his parents. Even tortoises. I decided to think them over in a nice long, hot shower but that reminded me that I'd left the magic soap in my room. I wasn't even sure where.

If Mom finds it she'll probably put it back in the bathroom again, I fretted. What if Penny washes her hair with it? Not likely, I decided, since she has about sixteen zillion bottles of shampoo, conditioner, rinse, and all-purpose goo. Besides, it might be cool if she did use it and turned up bald. But what if Mom uses it? Or Dad? I had to find that soap, then hide it and hide it good.

And I will, I promised myself. Right after breakfast. First things first.

Kathleen brought me plenty of rations. Her mom and dad were out and Uncle Terence was down in the basement and she had time to fill a small grocery sack. The grapes, on the bottom, were a little flat. It was a great effort though. I didn't complain. I tried to share the granola or at least some toast with Bumps. But Kathleen had to feed him. He wouldn't take it from the invisible kid. Not even with raspberry jam.

* * *

I shivered as Kathleen and I emerged into an overcast day that looked and definitely felt like rain was not far off. Bumps trotted out of the house with us and pranced about on the lawn, ignoring me. He let Kathleen scratch his ears but wouldn't come to me at all.

Well, I had more important problems: I had to figure out how to get into my house. We were half way there. "Kathleen, you knock on the door and tell my mom you came for my toothbrush. Tell her I didn't come because I was busy washing dishes at your house. I'll slip upstairs while the two of you are talking."

She glared at me. Actually, she glared a little to the left of me. "Your toothbrush? Washing dishes?" She laughed. "Get real. Who would believe that?"

"Okay, okay. We'll think of something else," I said.

"Maybe being invisible rots your mind," she said. "Or maybe your brain disappeared along with the rest of you. Or maybe you've lost your mind. Or maybe you never *had* a —"

"Well, since you already think I'm crazy, listen to this. For your information, there's a secret door in the wall of your basement. Your uncle goes through it and there's a glow or a fire or something on the other side."

"Babble, babble, babble," she said, trying to tune me out.

"Yep. I'd say there's a secret room down there," I said.

"For your information, that house has been in my family for a long time. It was my father's father's. There's no secret door in the basement."

"Maybe lots of secret rooms. A whole network of tunnels and —"

"And there's no secret rooms."

"How do you know?"

"I just do. I live there," she said, as if I might not know. "And anyway, it just couldn't be. Your imagination's getting —"

"Yeah, and I can't be invisible, right?" I gave that a minute to sink in. Then I hit her with, "Maybe that's why Uncle Terence spends so much time down there."

"What does Uncle Terence have to do with —"

"Who are you talking to, Kathleen?"

I couldn't believe it. Eddie Maskit had snuck up on us. I had to jump to one side to avoid getting run over as he braked his bike and skidded sideways to a stop next to Kathleen.

"I thought I heard Casey," he said. "Where is she, anyway?" He looked back with satisfaction at the long

black skid mark he'd created. He pointed at Bumps.
"Isn't that her dog?"

When will you stop asking questions? I wanted to
ask him. He's always doing that in school. Asking
questions to show how smart he is. Or just because he's
nosey.

"Yeah, that's him, isn't it? I remember because Casey
tried to get him to bite me once." He crouched down
and put out his hand. "Here, Bumpy," he said.

"Bumps," Kathleen mumbled.

"What?" he said. Another question! "Why does she
call him Bumpy? I'm surprised he doesn't bite *her*."

Bite him. Bite him, I commanded Bumps with a
secret mental command. Bumps licked his hand.

"It's *Bumps*," Kathleen said. "Bumps. Not Bumpy.
Bumps." She tapped her foot.

Way to go, Kathleen.

"Well then, where's Casey? He's always with her.
And who were you talking to? Yourself?" He laughed.

"No. Of course I wasn't talking to myself," Kathleen
sneered at him.

"It sounded like Casey, talking about a secret room."

Kathleen stopped tapping her foot, swept her gaze
across the leaden sky, then said in a much friendlier
tone, "Well it wasn't. I was just practicing my
ventriloquy."

"Ventrilo what?" Eddie asked.

Ventrilo what? I wondered.

"You know, practicing being a ventriloquist. I throw
my voice into something. Like . . . like that *telephone*

pole, over *there*," she said. "Then I talk like *Casey*, for example."

"I doubt it," Eddie said. I tiptoed over to the pole. "And why are you talking so funny?"

Kathleen ignored his nosey question. "I could do it, probably, right now if you don't believe me," she said.

"Do it then."

"I could."

"Good. Do it."

"I will," Kathleen threatened.

"I'm waiting," Eddie said.

"Hi, Casey. How are you doing?" Kathleen said to the telephone pole. Her voice was breathy. She was a little nervous.

"I'm fine, Kathleen," I answered.

Eddie gaped at the pole, too dumbfounded for once even to ask a question. Kathleen smiled. So did I.

"Uh, Eddie here was wondering, what's that you were saying about secret rooms?" she said.

"There're secret rooms everywhere," I said. "Life is mysterious." If only I had a camera, I could get a picture of Eddie's tonsils, I thought. Not that I wanted one. "Hi, Eddie," I said.

Eddie swallowed. "Hi," he said. "Hi, Casey." Then he said to Kathleen, "That was great. Your mouth doesn't move at all. And it sounds just like Casey. How do you do that?"

"I'm an impersonator, too," Kathleen improvised.

"You are? I never knew that. Who else can you do?"

"Who else?" Kathleen looked at the sky for another answer. "Who else?" she repeated. She needed help. That was obvious.

"I don't do anybody else," I said for her. "Just Casey." Kathleen was as surprised as Eddie to hear this news from the telephone pole.

"You do Casey impersonations, and ventriloquism?" Eddie asked. "At the same time?"

"You just heard it, didn't you? It's called ventriloquation," Kathleen said. "It's very difficult." It seemed to me Kathleen was getting a little out of control.

"You know what? I'm going to have a party," Eddie said. "Yeah. Tomorrow night. You could come and do your act."

"Well, maybe," Kathleen said.

What? I hot-footed it over to Kathleen, scattering a few pieces of roadside gravel with my first step.

"And bring Casey. She'd love it," Eddie said.

I crunched on her toe a little. Just enough to bring her back to reality. Eddie watched one of the small stones I'd kicked skitter to a stop against his bike tire. He smiled. "Come on. It'll be fun."

"Well" — I stepped again, harder — "ow!" Kathleen said.

"What?" Eddie asked.

"Ow'll . . . tell her about it," Kathleen said.

A clap of thunder ended the conversation. I was never so glad to get caught in a rainstorm. As Eddie zoomed down the rain-spotted sidewalk he called back to Kathleen, "By the way, it's going to be a masquerade party."

"Can you believe it?" I said to Kathleen when he was out of earshot. "A masquerade party. In June yet. We don't have to go." Lightning sizzled through the clouds. The rain intensified. "Or maybe we do. It would be fun to give Eddie a good scare."

"Come on, Casey, I'm getting wet," Kathleen said.

"Yeah, I'm freezing."

"Guess what? You're also visible again," she said.

I looked down. "I don't see anything."

"That's the problem. Your body's blocking the drops and they're running down your skin. You look like a hole in the rain."

Kathleen ran with me the rest of the way to my house, hiding me from view as best she could. I invited her in but she said she wanted to go home and change. And she did. Bumps seemed uncertain whether he wanted to come in with me or go with Kathleen. But when I opened the door and went in he followed, wagging his tail. What a change, I thought.

I closed the door, turned around and there was Mom, staring right at me.

"Casey," she said, "what in the world are you doing standing there dripping wet, and *naked*?"

⇌ Eight ⇋

I knew, of course, that I was standing there dripping wet and naked. I just wondered how Mom knew. I looked down.

"Oh my liver," I said, "I'm visible."

"That's one way of putting it," Mom said. "And to half the neighborhood. Don't you know that people can see you when you come to the door like that?"

"No, Mom. I mean, yes, Mom." I wondered what *she* had seen.

"It's only a screen door. It's not like you're invisible you know."

"Yes, Mom. I mean, no, Mom."

She tapped her forefinger against the side of her head. "Think before you jump out of the shower to answer the door."

I took a deep breath and let it out slowly. It could have been worse. A lot worse. But there was no point boring Mom with details.

"Yes, Mom," I promised meekly and headed for my room. Bumps followed me up, wagging his tail as though I were a long-lost friend. They say that animals don't smile but he was awfully close.

"Come right down after you get dressed, dear," she called up the stairs. "I need help in the kitchen. Some people from the office are coming for lunch."

I dried off and threw on a pair of jeans and a T-shirt just as a sneezing fit hit. I hate sneezing inside my shirt. The soap was on my bed. I couldn't remember if that was where I left it or not. I took it out of the box and the acrid odor of smoldering leaves hit me. It looked okay, though, and I didn't hear my sister screaming anywhere so I was pretty certain nobody had used it.

The phone rang. I tossed the soap on the bed and answered at the extension in the hall just outside my door. It was Kathleen.

"Guess what? I'm visible," I whispered.

"You mean like before, in the rain?"

"No, I mean visible. As in able to be seen with the eyes."

"As in normal?" she said.

"Yeah."

"That's good."

"I don't know." I sneezed. "I am glad to get some warm clothes on though, and Bumps sure likes me better this way."

"Me, too," she said. As if there was any doubt in my mind.

"Guess what else? My mom caught me at the door."

"What did she say?"

"She said she thinks I'm too old to answer the door naked." We both laughed. "I've got to help her now. I'll come over when I can. Keep an eye on Uncle Terence."

"I don't spy on my uncle," she said sternly.

"Uh-oh," I said. Bumps was rolling around on the magic soap. "Bumps, don't!"

Bumps ignored me. He put his shoulder down on the soap and did an enthusiastic back roll, just like he does when he finds a spot on the ground that smells especially awful. Then he jumped up and licked the bar like it was candy.

"No!" I shouted in my harshest whisper.

"What's the matter?" Kathleen said.

I dropped the phone and dashed into my room. "Bumps, don't eat that," I said. I pushed him away and grabbed the soap, careful not to touch the wet spot he'd made and maybe lose a few fingers. Holding the bar between thumb and forefinger I slid it into its box, the way a detective slips the murder weapon into a plastic bag.

"Casey! I need you down here," Mom yelled from below.

"What's going on, Casey?" Kathleen's small voice leaked from the telephone dangling in the hallway.

"I'm talking to Kathleen, Mom," I yelled back.

"Now, Cassandra Ann," Mom said.

I stuffed the soap under my mattress. "Can't talk now," I told Kathleen and hung up.

Mom was in the kitchen cutting up vegetables for a salad. She was all smiles to see me. "Set the table in the dining room will you, dear? Use the good china and glassware."

"Okay."

"By the way, who was at the door before?"

"At the door?"

"You remember. The door. The naked door."

"Oh. Yeah. Uh, nobody I could see."

"Lucky for you, too. Honestly, Casey, I don't understand what got into you." She laid tomato slices in a crimson arc along the edge of the plate. "When did you get home anyway? I didn't hear you come in."

"Oh, not long before you saw me," I said, and made a fast exit into the dining room. I sneezed again.

"Now see, you've got a cold starting. That's what happens when you run around the house with nothing on," she said. If that's how you catch a cold I should have pneumonia by now, I thought.

"How many people are coming?" I asked, reaching into the cabinet for the plates — my hands were gone! I looked up my sleeve and punched myself in the forehead. I definitely had something up my sleeve, only it was invisible.

"Five," Mom said, her voice too close.

I turned around. She was standing in the little archway that joins the kitchen and dining room. I was paralyzed. Why isn't she fainting? I wondered.

"Earth to Casey. Earth to Casey," she said in a simulated computer-simulated voice. "The five member Away Team is in transit. Estimated time of arrival: sixty-three seconds."

She put a plate into my hands — perfectly normal hands — and went back into the kitchen. I looked at the plate. I looked at my hands. For a split second they seemed to disappear again. Or did I blink? What was going on?

I set a speed record for table setting, all the while blinking on and off, like a faulty light. Now you see me, now you don't. I supposed I hadn't stabilized fully back to normal. Or was this my fate for the rest of my life?

As soon as I finished with the table I tried to escape to my room. But just when I got to the stairs the doorbell rang and Mom asked me to get it. What she said exactly was, "Casey, get the door. If you're still dressed, that is." Ha, ha. Mothers can be very funny.

Luckily, I was blinked on when I opened the door. Mom came in and there were lots of hellos, taking of raincoats and umbrellas, "lovely weather for ducks" talk, et cetera, et cetera. In the commotion I inched my way towards the stairs again. But what I saw stopped me cold. Goose bumps sprouted and I broke out in a sweat.

Down the stairs came a tail. A wagging little white-with-a-black-tip tail. Bumps' tail. He likes to be in on the action. But I couldn't let him this time. I rushed up the stairs, grabbed where I thought his body should be and scooped an angry, barking Bumps right off his feet. At the top I glanced back down. Everyone had gone into the dining room except for Mr. Bigelow, Mom's boss. He was staring up the stairs with his mouth hanging open. But then, Mom says he always looks like that.

I closed my door behind us, me and a tail floating in mid air a few inches above the floor. I looked at Bumps' tail. Well, this solves one mystery. Invisible kids cannot see each other. At least they can't see invisible dogs.

Maybe rolling in the soap made him invisible. But that couldn't be, I decided, because holding the dry soap doesn't affect me. Maybe after he licked the soap he licked his body, or maybe the magic absorbs through the tongue to the whole body. I thought of testing that theory myself, but it smelled too strange to even think about licking it. Besides, why didn't it affect his tail? I wondered. How should I know? I never took biology yet. Or magicology, either. I wasn't even absolutely sure the soap was what made us invisible in the first place. Maybe it was food additives. Or extraterrestrials. Maybe our imaginations had gotten the better of us.

"What happened to you, Bumps?" I said. But then my hand disappeared and reappeared a moment later. He might well be asking the same question of me. "We're a couple of disaster areas, aren't we?"

The best thing is to try and get invisible again myself, I decided. Invisibility isn't as easy as I thought and Kathleen will be furious with me when I don't show up at her door again but it seems ten times better than this blinking in and out. I'll be able to sneak into Dr. Poof and Madame F's trailer and get hold of Kevin's birth certificate and look for other documents, too. Ones that might explain all this. And while I'm at it, maybe I can find the secret room.

I sneezed again. With the cooler wet weather I would freeze to death with no clothes. Then a most spectacular thought flashed into my brain. Maybe I can wash my clothes with the soap and make *them* invisible, too.

I didn't know how long it took to get invisible so I timed myself. It was 12:15. I took a shower with the soap and washed Bumps' tail and rinsed a shirt, jeans, underwear, and a hooded rain jacket. And my canvas shoes, of course. Shoes would look awfully funny walking down the street by themselves.

Bumps' tail and I were gone at 12:37, the clothes a minute later. That pretty well solved the mystery of whether the soap had anything to do with invisibility!

I dried the clothes and, getting dressed, I learned another thing. There are a lot of holes in clothes and you never think about it but you have to put exactly the correct arm or leg or head into exactly the right hole or it just won't work.

Finally, fully clothed, warm and dry, Bumps in my arms, I tiptoed triumphantly down the stairs. Just as I was getting safely through the door I sneezed again, loud.

"Casey?" Mom called from the dining room.

I closed the door to an inch and called in, "See you later, Mom. I'm going over to Kathleen's. She said I can spend the night again." Well, I was pretty sure I could *get* her to say it.

"Well, get to bed early," Mom said. "And take care of that cold or it'll be the death of you." That's going a little far, I thought.

I rang the bell at Kathleen's house and immediately realized my mistake. When Uncle Terence opened the door I snuck in, still carrying Bumps. Uncle Terence sighed and closed the door. "Good day to you then," he said to the air as he padded back toward the basement.

Kathleen was in her room. She was not happy that she couldn't find me again and that Mr. Bumps was invisible, too. She put a ribbon around his neck so we wouldn't step, sit, or lie on him.

I was starving again. I raided the grocery sack Kathleen had brought earlier. "Tonight I'm going to search around the basement and the outside of your house until I find that secret room," I said, chomping away on celery loaded with cream cheese.

"That is absolutely gross and disgusting," Kathleen said.

"Why? That's what detectives do," I protested. "They detect things. And there seems to me to be plenty going on lately that needs detecting."

"I'm talking about the yuck in your mouth. I can see it for a while before it disappears. Until your juices get hold of it, I guess."

"I can't help it, Kathleen. I've got to eat, don't I?"

"After this lovely mastication demonstration I may never eat again."

I studied Kathleen's face. "You look kind of pale," I said. "You're not going to throw up, are you?" She didn't answer. She just kept watching my mouth and saying "Yuuckk" in a way that began to make *me* feel like throwing up. "Quit it, Kathleen. Turn around or something." She did. "So. Getting back to business, what do you think about my plan?"

"This is better." She half turned toward me as she spoke, but one look at me and she snapped her head away again, like she did with the TV when she tried to watch *Invasion of the Body Snatchers* with me. "No offense, Casey," she said.

"My plan, Kathleen. What do you think about my plan?"

"What plan?"

"To find the secret room," I said. "In your basement." I didn't say so to Kathleen but I also had a feeling that

52

I was going to find some kind of connection between the kidnapers and the secret room. I didn't know why, or what it could be. Maybe it was just that they were all very strange and mysterious.

"Count me out," she said.

"I never said I was counting you in," I said.

"Just watch out for the trenches and pipes in the back yard," she said. "We're having a sprinkler system installed. And watch out for Uncle Terence, too."

"What do you mean?" I asked.

"Oh, I don't know. He just seems even more distracted than usual. He goes around the house sighing a lot."

"Yeah, I noticed that," I said.

"And he's been spending a lot more time in the basement, so be careful if you go down there." I flashed on Uncle Terence at the wall, the strange things he'd been saying lately. Maybe *he* was the connection between the kidnapers and the secret room. "I don't want him or my mom or dad finding out they have an invisible kid in the house."

"Well, I'll only be invisible for about a day and a half, I figure. The first time I used the soap I went to bed and woke up invisible and stayed that way until about eleven o'clock today. This morning I found out it takes about twenty or twenty-five minutes for the soap to work. So I was invisible for about one and a half days. I'm guessing it will last that long again. Which means I've got all night tonight and all day tomorrow until midnight to get a lot of detecting work done."

"Don't tell me about it, please," Kathleen said.

"But don't you think we should find out about Kevin?" I hoped that would entice her.

She mulled it over. "Well, maybe it would be good to make sure Dr. Poof and Madame F are his parents."

"Of course they're not his parents," I huffed. "I told you, I saw the birth certificate and it said Kevin Spelling. Haven't you been paying attention?" I think I kind of annoyed her.

"I'm not speaking to you, Casey Granger," Kathleen said. And she didn't. I was glad when her mother finally called her for dinner. While she was gone Bumps and I ate some lunch. He loved the peanut butter crackers. I could tell by the noise he made trying to get it off the roof of his mouth.

That night I went to bed early. Kathleen said I almost looked like a real person once I got under the covers. Bumps made his nest at the end of the bed, pushing up against my feet. I set my mental alarm clock for one a.m.

When I woke up I could hear Kathleen's rhythmic breathing. Bumps snuck out the door with me. I guess he didn't mind me being invisible so much now that he was, too. But his ribbon was a dead giveaway if anybody saw it. I took it off.

The basement was empty. I went to the back wall. I looked again for cracks, hinges, loose blocks, a hidden button. When I couldn't find any I gave up and went outside to see if I could find a door in.

It was drizzling. Clouds and fog swallowed up any light there might have been. The first thing I did was trip over a pipe. Apparently I'd detected the sprinkler system. I hunted for the secret entry around some very wet bushes at the back of the house.

Before long I was cold again. Clothes don't help much when they're soaked. I was ready to give up. But then I thought I caught a glint of golden light a few feet out from the house. I felt my way around loose pipe and over shallow ditches toward the ever-brightening shaft of light. The closer I got the more it seemed to be coming out of the ground itself. It must be a work light of some kind, left in one of the trenches by the sprinkler people, I thought. Maybe the rain shorted it out. I hope I don't get electrocuted. My body'll be hard to find.

The light was right in front of me now, seeping softly from a narrow crevice in the earth. I took another step. The ground gave way beneath me.

I was falling.

⇌ Nine ⇋

I landed in a heap on a hard dirt surface. Bumps barked somewhere up above. "Quiet, Bumps. I'm okay," I said. I rubbed my hip and shoulder. "I think." I rubbed some more and looked around. It was pretty easy to see, really, because of the glow from the gold.

The glow from the gold?!

I jumped to my feet, forgetting all about bruised muscles and possible broken bones. A large pot full to overflowing with gold coins sat squarely in the center of the room. I plunged my hands in wrist deep. The coins felt warm as bath water. And I felt a pressure, a light throbbing against my fingers like a timid pulse. It gave me an eerie feeling, almost as if the gold were alive, but it was strangely comforting, too. I picked up one of the coins and slipped it into my pocket to get a good look later.

The chamber I was in was about as big as my bedroom. It had a dirt floor, a dirt ceiling supported by boards and heavier beams and posts, and dirt walls — except for one, which was made of concrete blocks like the basement wall. And it was empty, except for the gold and me. I was sure I was in the secret room and that the concrete wall was the one Uncle Terence had come through from the basement. The pot of gold explained the glow I'd seen as Uncle Terence came through the wall. Except I'd never heard of gold that glows.

The concrete wall felt solid. What else was new? I ran my hands over every inch of it but I couldn't find any secret latches, knobs, or catches to open it from this side any more than I had from the other. Since I couldn't find any mechanical way to open the door, I decided to try some magic words. I said, "Abracadabra." It didn't work. I said it slow. I said it fast. I said it three times without stopping. It still didn't work. "Open sesame" was useless, too. I tried "In-a-gadda-da-vida," which does something for my dad about once a year when he plays it on the stereo but, I found out, does nothing for concrete walls. I even tried "Monkey see, monkey do." Nothing happened.

All the while I was doing these things rain was sprinkling through the hole above. The floor was getting slippery and small puddles were forming in the low spots. The hood of my jacket was beginning to soak through. A trickle of water ran down my spine. I kicked the wall. My motto is, if at first you don't succeed, try kicking. But that didn't accomplish anything either, except for getting me a sore foot.

Okay, I decided, if I can't get out this way I'll get out the way I got in. I looked up at the hole in the ceiling. Bumps was still up there. I could hear him whining. The ragged opening I'd fallen through was several feet out of reach. It took several tries but I finally was able to climb up on the pot and reach from there but even then my fingers just grazed the ground above. I could reach high enough to send tiny avalanches of mud and wood from rotted ceiling supports tumbling into my nose and eyes, but not high enough to pull myself out.

Out of the corner of my watery left eye I saw a blurry shadow. I looked, and saw the concrete wall, fuzzy and out of focus. Then I saw part of Uncle Terence. Then I saw all of him, standing right there in the secret room with me. I was so shocked I almost fell off the pot.

"Well, look who's come a-callin'," he said.

"Hi, Uncle Terence," I said, as though meeting up with him when I was invisible in a secret room full of gold after he just walked through a wall was an everyday occurrence. "I just dropped in for a minute. I've got to go now."

Uncle Terence looked at his watch. "Let's see, 1:40. I suppose it would be just a little after your bed time, wouldn't it?" I kept straining to reach the ground above and pull myself out of there. Bumps licked my fingers and barked. "My, my. We do have a problem," he said. "Seems the ceiling's sprung quite a leak. Come on down from there, Casey, darlin', before you hurt yourself."

"I didn't mean to break in," I said, jumping down from the pot.

"Oh, you didn't now?" He didn't look angry; more like he was enjoying himself, in fact. I decided to level with him.

"Well I *was* kind of snooping but I didn't mean to hurt anything. I'm a detective," I added, hoping that might excuse something. "How did you know I was here? I'm invisible."

"So, you're invisible, are you? Well," his eyes twinkled almost as much as the gold itself, "it just so happens that your invisible dog was barking outside my bedroom window. And it also just so happens that there's a shiny gold coin in your invisible pocket."

I reached into my pocket, my face warming and probably getting very red if anyone could have seen it. "Here." I held the coin out. It appeared to hang between us. "I guess this is yours, huh?"

"No. It's yours. My gift to you. No one's ever found the gold before," he said. "You must be a pretty good detective." His eyes twinkled again.

"I knew this was a secret room! I knew it. I knew it," I said, bouncing around the room like I was on a runaway pogo stick. "Kathleen wouldn't believe me, but I knew it." I stopped bouncing. "But how did you get in, Uncle Terence? I couldn't find any door, inside or out. And I used all the magic commands I could think of."

"Well you see, only I know how to get in. Officially, that is." He eyed the damaged cave roof. "Although you did find your own very creative entrance. But you couldn't get through that wall." He thumped the wall with his balled up fist, showing me what I already knew: that it was rock solid. "Not by yourself."

Which didn't exactly answer my question.

He looked up at the hole again. "Something's got to be done about that or the sprinkler men will be dropping in, too. And that won't do." He took a crisply folded piece of white cloth from his hip pocket and wiped the rain off his face. "I'll tell you what, darlin', let's continue our talk someplace more comfortable. And dry.

59

I'll hoist you up through the hole. You collect Mr. Bumps and meet me in the hall outside my bedroom. Agreed?"

"Agreed," I said, "except I don't think you can lift me, can you, Uncle Terence?" I hoped I didn't hurt his feelings.

"Well, let's see," he said, and before I knew it he'd grabbed me under the arms and swung me onto his shoulders as easily as if he were putting on a jacket. "Lock your legs behind me," he said, and stepped lightly up onto the lip of the pot. Uncle Terence was stronger than he looked. There seemed to be a lot about Uncle Terence that I didn't know.

My head was at ground level. I grabbed wet grass and dug my fingers into the mud and I pulled and strained. Then a mighty shove from below sent me sprawling on the wet ground. I lurched to my feet, just in time to fall over Mr. Bumps. I slithered toward the hole, wondering how Uncle Terence was going to get out and hoping maybe to get a peek at him going through that wall.

But I didn't see him. In fact, I couldn't even find the hole! And it wasn't the dark. The clouds had broken and moonlight made it easy to see. There simply was no hole, no gold, no Uncle Terence.

Nothing.

⇌ Ten ⇌

Detective intuition told me not to waste any more time looking. I sprang to my feet, hurdled the sprinkler piping, dashed in the back door and through the kitchen and careened down the hall toward the basement. Too late: Uncle Terence was waiting for me at his bedroom.

"Here I am," I said. He smiled, and pointed to the coin in my pocket. "Oh. Yeah." I took the coin out. I put it in the other pocket, which didn't help. "How did you get here?" I asked. "What happened to the hole?" I sounded like Eddie Maskit.

"Why don't we talk inside," Uncle Terence said.

It was a small room with a small bed, two overstuffed chairs and a wall full of photographs. Uncle Terence went into his bathroom and came back with a towel for drying Bumps. "Do you have some string or something?" I asked. "That way we can see him better."

Uncle Terence disappeared into the bathroom again and returned with a piece of dental floss which he tied around Bumps' chest. I sat in one of the large comfortable chairs and Uncle Terence took the other. For a few minutes we just sat, watching Bumps' string float around the room. Judging by the frequent stops and starts of the string, and the occasional dog snorts, he

61

was sniffing everything, sorting things out. That's what I needed to do. Sort things out, I mean.

"Did you know I was at the door today? Yesterday, that is," I said, "when you answered the bell and there was no one there?"

"I did."

"And when you said 'Good day to you' you weren't just being Uncle Terence? I mean, you were actually talking to me?"

"I was."

"But how did you know I was there? I was invisible, wasn't I? And I didn't have this." I touched the coin, startled again by its warmth and pulse.

"I didn't know," Uncle Terence said. "But I had a pretty strong hunch *some*body was around. Doorbells don't ring by themselves."

"But an invisible kid? Is that your first guess when nobody's at the door?"

He smiled. "Not normally. But you'll recall you have been asking some fairly strange and pointed questions recently about invisible trailers and hammers and shoes. I tried ignoring your questions and then gave you unasked for advice instead. Two very bad strategies. I guess I hoped you would just forget about what you saw." He humped his shoulders apologetically. "Not likely, huh?"

"Probably not," I agreed.

"So I concluded. And, knowing something about your determination and curiosity and sense of adventure, and having had similar experiences myself, I just put two and two together." That amused expression filled his face again. "Besides, when I opened the door I could hear Bumps. He pants when you hold him."

"What do you mean, similar experiences?" I said.

"Well, let's just say we buy our soap at the same market."

"Aha! Dr. Poof and Madame Farsight," I said. "So you were invisible that day in the basement. *You* were swinging that hammer." For a moment it seemed like I had solved something. It was a short moment. "But why?" I asked. "Why be invisible just to work in your own shop? And risk getting caught?"

"I didn't mean to," he said.

"Be invisible or get caught?"

"Both. You see, I thought I was visible. But it doesn't wear off all at once. It comes and goes."

"Tell me about it," I agreed.

"Well, one minute I'll be perfectly —"

"I know," I said. "I know. It's happened to me, too."

"Oh. Then why did you want me to tell you about it?"

"I didn't." It took me a minute to figure out what he was talking about. "Oh. 'Tell me about it.' That means 'I already know about it,'" I explained.

"So it means '*don't* tell me about it'?"

"You got it, Uncle Terence."

"And that means . . ."

"That means 'you got it'." We laughed.

But my laugh was cut short. I'd forgotten about Kevin. He still needed my help. "Do you know they kidnaped a little boy, Uncle Terence? Dr. Poof and Madame F, I mean? His name's Kevin. Kevin Spelling.

But they're name's not Spelling and he doesn't look like them at all and I found his birth certificate with his real parents' names, so I can prove it and —"

Uncle Terence interrupted with another laugh, a merry chuckle that didn't fit my tale of kidnaping. "No, you've got it all wrong. You don't have to worry about Kevin. He's their little boy all right."

"But —"

"I know that for a fact," he said in a serious tone.

It's hard not to believe Uncle Terence, he's so sincere. And I've never known him to tell a lie. But I felt just as sure that there was more he wasn't telling me. I decided to try a different approach.

"Where did Dr. Poof and Madame Farsight get the soap?" I asked, sounding like Eddie Maskit again.

"I can't talk about that, Casey," he said. "That's their business. Maybe they'll tell you all about it someday. But until they do, I suggest you stay away from that trailer. And stay visible."

"Uh-oh. Isn't that giving advice?" I kidded. But Uncle Terence didn't kid back.

"Listen now. If you know there's danger up ahead and you see someone headed that way, do you tell them or do you wait to be asked?"

"I'd tell," I said.

"Me, too."

"But there's a lot of things I don't understand," I said. "Why are you invisible sometimes, and how about the secret room?" I thought only Eddie asks two questions in the same sentence. "And you never told me how you get in and out."

"Well," he murmured, "that's *my* business." He looked off into the room at nothing in particular and didn't say another word. It seemed like our talk was over.

All I noticed after that was how drowsy I felt and how soft and comfy that big chair was. Maybe I fell asleep. Then Uncle Terence was saying, "Would you like a little something to eat before you go to bed?" That woke me up.

"Food? Sure."

While he was gone I studied the photographs, which covered half of one wall and most of another. There were no people in any of the pictures. Just lots of green meadows and fields separated by low stone walls. One of the pictures, blown up poster size, was of an old house. It was made of stone, too. Everything looked green and fresh and alive. Even the stones. There must have been a million of them.

Uncle Terence came back with some apple cider and cookies on a tray. He poured something I guessed was whiskey into his cider. "Did you take these pictures?" I asked.

"I did. On my trip to Ireland." He told me that his grandfather, Shamus O'Toole, was born in Ireland. "In that very house," he said, pointing to the poster. "When my great-grandfather died Shamus came to the United States."

"With the gold?" It was a pure guess.

"Yes," he said. "With the gold. His son — my father — married an Irish-American lass, and they had two children. Kathleen's father, and me."

"Did your grandfather dig that secret room to keep the gold?" I asked.

"Yes," he said. "That he did."

"Where did he get it in the first place?"

"I can't rightly say, Casey. It's been in my family as long as anyone can remember," he said.

"So you and Kathleen's father inherited the gold when your father died?"

"No," he said. "*I* inherited the gold."

"Just you?" He nodded. "Why just you?" I had the sudden feeling I was minding someone else's business again.

"It's just the way of things, Casey," he said. "Just the way of things."

I took the coin out of my pocket and looked at it. "Gosh," I said.

"Gosh what?"

"I've never known a rich person before."

"You've known *me* before, haven't you?" he said. He had me there. "Actually, though, I'm not so rich as you seem to think. That gold is not what it appears to be."

"What do you mean? What is it?"

"Well, anyone might think a pot of gold would make you happy. But I tell you, that gold — and all that goes with it — has been a millstone around my neck."

I didn't know what a millstone was but it didn't sound good, especially around the neck. "Well then, why don't you get rid of the gold? Use it for something," I said.

"What do you have in mind?"

66

I thought for a moment. "Maybe for a dream. A secret dream of something you always wanted but couldn't have. If I had a lot of money I'd open a detective agency."

He flashed me a grin, then just as suddenly frowned and looked down at his glass. "That's a fine sounding idea, Casey. But it's more complicated than that."

"How?"

"For one thing, no one's ever used the gold before. It's come down to me intact through many generations. Hundreds and hundreds of years."

I tried to imagine hundreds and hundreds of years. I knew Mom was thirty-eight. Her grandma, who was my great grandma, died two years ago. I think she was eighty-nine, which, except for having known her myself, was older than I could imagine. That wasn't even one hundred years, but it was about as far as I could go. "But what's the good of it if you can't use it?" I asked Uncle Terence.

"That's a reasonable question. Still, hundreds of years and many generations is a long time. I feel a responsibility to preserve it."

"So you can pass it on to Kathleen?" Uncle Terence didn't have any children.

"No. It cannot go to her. Only to certain people." That sounded mysterious. "I hoped that I would find someone in Ireland, but . . ." He looked old and sad all of a sudden. Then he brightened for an instant, looking at me through half-closed eyes. "Use it for a dream, you say." His smile broadened. "That's a fine thought, my girl. A fine thought."

Uncle Terence swallowed the last of his cider. He hadn't had any cookies, just his drink. When I finished off the last one a minute later he was sound asleep in his chair. I picked up Bumps and slipped out.

My mind was churning on the way back to Kathleen's room. I hadn't had a chance to compare notes with Uncle Terence about being invisible or to ask him why the gold glows and feels warm. I never noticed Mom's gold ring or watch glowing or feeling warm. I had a hunch the stuff in the secret room wasn't gold at all. But what else could it be? How did Uncle Terence get hold of the soap anyway? And what was his connection with Dr. Poof and Madame Farsight? He was sure quick to defend them about Kevin. I was suspicious of that. Maybe they were blackmailing him or something. I decided to keep the Kevin case open.

There were so many unanswered questions, and they all seemed tied in with Uncle Terence. I had a feeling there was a lot that he was trying to hide. I felt a little sorry for him. He couldn't hide his unhappiness. He reminded me of the tortoise in Madame Farsight's story. The tortoise, she had said, "does not want to be known. She hides inside her shell and thinks she is invisible." Come to think of it, maybe there was more than one tortoise around. I put my coin under the pillow and fell asleep thinking about Ireland and tortoises and gold.

*　*　*

I woke late. Ten a.m. I had been dreaming that Dr. Poof and Uncle Terence were arguing about the pot of gold, tugging it back and forth between them. Then, as I came all the way awake, I found I really was hearing raised voices.

"No, Mom, don't come in. I'll change the sheets," Kathleen said in a loud voice.

"I need them for the wash, Katie. I want to do them now." I could tell she meant business. "And why are you shouting?"

"I'm taking them off right now," Kathleen said, pulling at her bedding. She sounded desperate. And she was still shouting.

I rolled out of bed as nimbly as any Good Guy dodging the Bad Guy's knife, grabbing Bumps along the way. I pulled off his marker string and stood in the corner with him. Out of the way, I hoped.

Mrs. O'Toole walked in. "What's going on, Katie?" She studied the room. "How did you mess up both beds?" she asked. She came right over to mine and flung the bedspread to the floor.

That's when I remembered my gold coin under the pillow.

⇌ Eleven ⇋

Before I could move, Kathleen's mom grabbed
the sheets from one side, snapped her wrists with the
strength and precision of a martial arts master, and
whisked the sheets off the bed so fast that the pillow
didn't even move.

It took me a microsecond or two to realize I had a
second chance. And it would have taken several more
microseconds for my brain to formulate and send
instructions to my muscles to make an invisible lunge
for the coin. But it didn't matter. Because long before
that Mrs. O'Toole whipped the pillow from its place,
stripped it of its pillowcase skin, and left it in a soft
lump at the foot of the bed. A moment ago it seemed
bad enough that she should find the coin. But, staring at
the striped and dimpled surface of the naked mattress, I
saw that the reality was worse: my coin wasn't there!

My eyes scanned the floor like a prison spotlight.
Then I was down on my hands and knees. I wasn't
thinking about being cautious and quiet. I was thinking
about finding that coin. By some grace, Mrs. O'Toole
avoided colliding with me.

When she left, her arms full of sheets, Kathleen sat
down on her bed and held her head in her hands. "That
was close. Boy, that was close," she said. "That was

really close." I didn't offer any sympathy. Someone had stolen my gold coin.

"Kathleen," I blurted with the urgency of the recently robbed. My disembodied voice didn't even make her flinch.

"Boy, that was close," she said again.

"Kathleen, I've got to tell you something."

"Don't bother me," she said.

"But this —"

She leveled a killer look right at me. Somehow. "You're bothering me," she said, baring her teeth malevolently.

I couldn't let that bother me. "This is important," I said.

"Oh, I know it's important, Casey. I know. Everything you do is important." Her words came out fast and hard. She paced around the room like a wild animal, like Lon Chaney, Jr. always did just before he turned into *The Wolf Man.* "But I guess it's not important that I was arguing like an idiot with my mom for half an hour, is it?" I had to keep moving to keep from getting trampled. "And it's not important that I almost had a heart attack when she came in the room." Maybe my imagination was getting the better of me, but I'd never noticed what big, sharp teeth Kathleen has. "And I guess it's not important that now my mother thinks I'm crazy because I sleep in both beds!"

"But you don't understand," I said to the Wolf Girl.

"Sure I do, Casey," she snarled. "It's simple. Nobody's important but *you.* Nothing's important but

71

what *you* do. That covers it, doesn't it?" If she could have, she would have tapped both feet.

"Okay, okay," I said, still jumping around to keep out of her path. "I get the point."

"Good. So don't talk to me. Here." She scooped several handfuls of cornflakes out of her pocket and threw the little crushed bits of cereal on the bed. "Eat."

Kathleen is not a cornflakes-on-the-bed sort of person.

But I didn't eat. Instead, I rooted through the blanket. I shook the pillow. I lifted the mattress. I peered under the bed.

"What do you think you're doing, Casey?"

I shook the throw rug that lay between the beds. "I'm not supposed to talk," I said.

"*Now*, Cassandra Ann Granger, you *are* supposed to talk." She sounded pretty sure.

"I lost the coin," I said.

"What coin? Stop shaking the rug. You're spreading dust."

"Where did your mom take the sheets?"

"To a movie, where do you think? Stop it." She grabbed the rug from me, put it on the floor and stood on it.

"The laundry's in the basement, right?" I sounded a little hysterical to me.

"Why? What's going on?"

"You keep Bumps. Don't let him out of here." I didn't wait for any objections.

On my way to the basement I almost ran down Mrs. O'Toole who was on her way up the narrow steps. I back-pedaled to the top, matching the noise of my footsteps with hers as best I could, and let her slip past. Kathleen would have been really mad if I knocked her mother down the stairs. And Mrs. O'Toole wouldn't have been so happy about it, either.

Downstairs, the washer was running and a pile of sheets was on the floor. I looked through them. No coin. I turned off the washer and tugged at the sheets inside. They were heavy, and I splattered the whole area searching through them. I plunged my arm in deep and walked my fingers in a circle around the hole-pocked bottom. Nothing. I sank to the floor in despair. How could everything go so wrong just since last night?

Oh my liver! Uncle Terence! He would know what was going on!

I rushed up the stairs and tiptoed down the hall to his room. I knocked softly. There was no answer. I put my ear to the door and listened, but there was nothing to hear. I cupped my hands around my mouth and leaned against the door. "Uncle Terence," I said, pushing my voice through the wood. I listened again. The place was quiet as a church on Tuesday. I looked up and down the hall. No one was in sight. I turned the knob and let myself in, closing the door with a barely audible *click* behind me.

I looked around the small room. The bed was neatly made, the bathroom was unoccupied, the closet was open.

And empty.

⇌ Twelve ⇌

"Your uncle's not in his room. I think something's wrong," I told Kathleen when I got back.

"How do you know he's not in his room? Maybe he's sleeping. Or showering."

"He's not sleeping or showering."

"How do you know?"

"Because I was *in* his room," I said. "He's not there."

Kathleen looked at me as though I had just pawned her mom's wedding ring for pizza money. "You were in Uncle Terence's room when he wasn't there?"

"Well, yes. But it was for a good reason," I said.

"What good reason?"

"To . . . to find out . . . something."

"Find out . . . what?" she wanted to know.

"To find out if he was there! Kathleen, you're missing the point. Which is that Uncle Terence is gone. His clothes are gone."

"His clothes? All of them?"

"Yes. Did he go on one of his trips or something?"

"I don't know," she said, and ran out the door. Now it was my turn to be left behind. I paced. I ate cornflake crumbs. But my heart wasn't in it. I offered them to Bumps. He was still going at them when Kathleen came back. "You're right. He's gone. Mom showed me the note he left." She held up a yellow square of paper.

Back when you see me.
Not to worry.   -T.

was printed in neatly formed letters on two lines. The
other side was blank.

"That's it?" I asked. Kathleen nodded. "Why didn't
your mom say anything about the note before, when she
came in this morning?"

Kathleen shrugged. "I think she's embarrassed about
it or something. Maybe she's worried." She sighed. "I
just hate when he does this," she said. "No goodbye or
anything." She sat heavily on the bed. Her eyes looked
wet. I sat, too. "He could be hit by a bus or drown in a
river or fall off a mountain and I'd never see him
again," she said. "I don't even know where he went."

"Ireland probably," I said. "He'll be all right. And
he'll be back, too, Kathleen." I put my arm around her
shoulders and jostled her to buck her up. The mirror on
her dresser showed Kathleen alone on the bed, slumping
to the side and jiggling like a rag doll in a miniature
earthquake.

"Ireland?" she asked.

"Could be," I said. "He has a lot of pictures."

"Casey, you're not making any sense."

I jostled her some more. "Look," I said, pointing at
the mirror. We both laughed.

The blare of a radio drew me to the window. The sun
peeked past the edge of a cloud and two men from the
sprinkler company were unloading their gear in the yard.
I picked up the flashlight Kathleen always keeps by her

bed. "Kathleen," I said, "watch Bumps again for me will you?"

"Hold it," she said. "If this is about Uncle Terence, I'm coming with you." She grabbed the flashlight from me. "And if we're leaving this room I think I'd better carry this. You take Bumps," she ordered. I did.

On the way I grabbed a shovel from the garage, handed it to Kathleen, and led her around the far side of the house, avoiding the workmen.

"Where are we going?" Kathleen asked.

"To find Uncle Terence, maybe," I said.

"What's the flashlight for? It's broad daylight."

"You'll see." A minute later we were standing on perfectly ordinary-looking grass, over what I was sure was Uncle Terence's perfectly extraordinary hiding place. "Dig here," I told Kathleen. Kathleen put the point of the shovel to the ground, then stopped and looked at me.

"Why?" she said in a voice so small and shaky I could barely hear. But it was her face, pale and full of fear, that made me understand.

"I didn't mean *that*," I said. "He's not dead. This is his secret room, under here." I patted the ground. "The one I told you about."

Kathleen dug, even though I could tell she still didn't believe me about the room. On the fifth or sixth shovelful she hit something. I held onto Bumps with one hand and dug into the loose dirt with the other, found the boards, and then a little crack between them.

"What is it?" Kathleen said, down on her knees beside me now. I turned the flashlight on and poked it between two boards. I don't know what I expected to find. Not Uncle Terence — why would he take all his clothes to a hole in the ground? I just thought I should look. Maybe to convince myself that it hadn't all been a dream last night. The spindly beam of light darted around the little room.

"What is it?" Kathleen said again. "Let me see."

"Just a minute. Just a minute." I couldn't believe what I was seeing. Uncle Terence wasn't there. But neither was the pot of gold! The room was totally empty. I sat back in a daze. "Here," I said, handing the flashlight to Kathleen.

"Holy cow!" she said. "It is a room or something, just like you said. But it's empty. Where's Uncle Terence?"

"He's not there," I said.

"But where is he?" she insisted.

"I don't know. Yet. We'd better cover this up and get out of here."

We pushed the dirt back. We retraced our steps, put the shovel back in its place. On the way back to Kathleen's room I tried to make sense out of everything.

First my coin was missing. Then Uncle Terence was missing. Now the whole pot of gold was missing. Maybe Uncle Terence disappeared with both my coin and the pot of gold. But that idea raised more questions than it answered. Where would he go and why would he take the gold? And what about my coin? Had he snuck into Kathleen's room and taken it? After he said it was mine to keep? Was he mad at me? Maybe he didn't trust me. Maybe my snooping had caused him to leave for good this time. That thought really bothered me.

When we got back to her room Kathleen said, "Casey, you're here. You're all here I mean. I can see you."

I looked at myself. She was right. "But this is way too soon," I said. The clock on Kathleen's chest of drawers said 11:50. "About twelve hours too soon." I picked up the clock and shook it. The glow-red numbers danced and shimmied, but when I set it down and the dancing was done, it still said 11:50. Bumps ran over and rubbed against my leg. "Look. Bumps is back, too," I said.

"Good."

"Kathleen, I've got to go over to the lot to check something out," I said. "Want to come with me?"

Kathleen shook her head. "I don't think so, Casey. I've had about all I can handle for one morning. Besides, maybe Uncle Terence will show up. Or call."

"Okay. Talk to you later."

On my way out the front door I met Mrs. O'Toole. "Hi, Casey," she said. "Nice to see you. I didn't know you were here."

"Good. I mean, it's good to see you, too, Mrs. O'Toole. I've got to go now."

Mr. Bumps and I ran all the way to the lot. I didn't see the trailer. I walked to about where I thought it should be. Then I inched forward, my arms stretched out in front of me so I wouldn't run into it like I did the last time. I moved to the right. I moved to the left. But I didn't come up with anything. I kept searching around, like I do sometimes when I lose something — I look in the place where I think it should be over and over even though I know it's not there, because I don't know what else to do. And the thought kept going through my mind: first the coin, then Uncle Terence, then the pot of gold. And now the trailer. There seemed to be a pattern emerging!

"What are you doing, Casey?" I jumped and turned at the sound of the familiar voice. It was Eddie Maskit. Didn't I have enough trouble without him sticking his nose in? "You look pretty silly walking around like that," he said. "You look like Frankenstein." He put his arms out in front of him and walked stiff-legged towards me.

"Well you look pretty silly, too, Eddie. Why don't you go home now, and look silly there?" I said.

"What are you looking for?" he asked, dropping the Frankenstein bit. I ignored him. He bent down and started poking at the ground. "Look at this, Casey. A lot of dead grass here. Kind of in a rectangle shape."

All the while I'd been feeling in the air for it, the evidence was there on the ground. This was the right spot. The trailer had yellowed the grass here.

"What do you think?" Eddie asked.

I thought three things: the trailer had been in this spot; the trailer wasn't here now; and if it was invisible, it could be just about anywhere.

"I don't think anything," I said. I picked up Bumps, who was smelling around the dead grass, and started walking away, fast. "Bye, Eddie. See you around."

"Tonight," he said. "At my party."

I stopped and turned. "Tonight?" In all the excitement I'd forgotten about it.

"I will see you there, won't I? I told you about it day before yesterday. Remember?"

"Yeah, I remember." Eddie's eyebrows arched and a little smile appeared. "I remember now," I said. "You told Kathleen. She was talking about it yesterday." Whew. That was close.

Eddie's grin faded a little. "So you're coming? I have a feeling it won't be any fun without you."

I turned around and walked again, faster. "I don't know," I stalled, trying to retreat out of earshot. "I might be busy."

"Oh come on. Kathleen won't do her act unless you're there."

I looked over my shoulder. Eddie was just standing there, watching me. Even from that distance I could tell he was trying to stare me down. Fat chance. Then his mouth moved, and a split-second later two words leaped the distance between us.

"Will she."

It wasn't a question.

⇌ Thirteen ⇋

My parents were having a party that night themselves. And since Penny was working at the bakery I got an exclusive opportunity to help with the housework. Poor Penny, sampling cheesecake and sweet rolls — having to be paid for it — while I got to wash dishes. For free! Clean the bathroom, too. Run the vacuum from one end of the house to the other. But just when I thought I would faint from fun, Mom said I had to quit.

"Aw, Mom."

"No whining," she said, playing along.

"Well, gee, could I at least clean up after the party?"

"You'll probably hate this, but I was thinking maybe you could spend the night at Kathleen's. If it's okay with the O'Tooles."

Perfect. "Do I have to?"

"I could save some dirty dishes for you."

"Well . . ."

"Maybe plug up the disposal."

"Well . . . okay then."

I retreated to my room. I pulled the soap out from under the mattress and, with the joyful feeling that only impending revenge can bring, planned what I was going to do to scare Eddie. I hoped Kathleen wasn't still angry. I called her and asked about staying over.

"That depends," she said.

She was.

I explained that it was my mom's idea. "It would be like doing her a favor," I said. Kathleen likes my mom. Last year she even sent my mom a birthday card, which made me look bad, since I forgot. But Kathleen is not a person easily distracted.

"Will you be visible or invisible?" she asked. "Let me rephrase that. Normal or abnormal?"

"Well, that's hard to know," I said.

"No it's not. You were visible when you left here a few hours ago. To the uninformed you probably appeared to be a relatively normal human being. I just want to know, do you plan to stay that way or not?"

"But it's not working like I thought it would," I reminded her. "I could disappear at any time." Which was true, technically.

"Well, then I'll see you when you *are* normal. Which may take years in your case." She hung up.

I redialed. "Don't forget, Eddie's party's tonight," I said, trying a new tack. There was a short silence.

"I don't have to go to his party. I'm not even the one who likes Eddie Maskit." What was that supposed to mean? The line went dead.

I dialed again. "Come on, Kathleen. That's the point. We'll have a lot of fun teasing smart alec Eddie and his stuck up friends."

"No." Another dial tone.

There was only one strategy left. Guilt. I stabbed the redial button again. "But you already promised Eddie you'd come."

"I don't care. You've been getting me involved in stuff I never ever wanted to get involved in, Casey Granger."

"Me?"

"I never wanted an invisible friend, for example. I never wanted to get stuck in a carnival trailer, either, listening to mumbo jumbo. And I never wanted to sneak an invisible kid and dog into and out of my house, steal food for them, and get into trouble because *you* left a wet mess all over the laundry room."

I almost interrupted once or twice to argue a few points but decided to hold my tongue and let her get it all off her chest. "Okay," I said when she seemed to have finished. "How about this? If I promise to leave you out of any future invisible adventures, after tonight, will you go to Eddie's party with me and let me sleep over afterwards, whether I'm invisible or not?"

"Well . . ."

"Staying over was my mom's idea," I reminded her. I waited, holding my breath.

"There's one other thing," she said.

"What?"

"What about Uncle Terence?"

"What about him?"

"Maybe it slipped your microscopic mind, Casey. He's missing, remember? And this time I think it has something to do with you and all your nosing around. You're just like Eddie."

Guilt and Eddie Maskit thrown at me in the same breath? I didn't like it one bit. "It's not my fault he's gone, Kathleen. Come on. This is Uncle Terence we're talking about. Sometimes he goes away. Anyhow, there's nothing we can do tonight. But I promise we'll get on it again tomorrow. If he's not already back."

Again there was a silence at the other end of the line. "Okay then."

"Great. Now here's the plan. Tonight after supper I'll use the soap and come on over to your house. We'll figure out our act and make costumes. Then we'll go over to Eddie's."

"Okay," she said limply.

I wasn't going to let Kathleen's lack of enthusiasm stop me. I had plans. Plans that were going to scare the nose right off The Nosey Boy's face.

*   *   *

After supper I washed with the soap, got dressed, and started out the bedroom door. Bumps whined and barked. I explained that I couldn't take him to the party and I couldn't leave him alone at Kathleen's, either. I don't think he understood, or maybe he just didn't want to. With a scowl on his furry face he watched me go.

At Kathleen's we improvised a standard ventriloquism act. Minus the dummy, of course. "After that, you go into a trance like Madame Farsight and say that you feel the presence of a poltergeist in the room. I'll blink the light on and off and move things through the air. Then I'll appear in that old cloak of your mom's. When they're scared out of their costumes I'll just fade away into the night. I'll wait for you by that hedge that runs alongside Eddie's driveway."

84

Kathleen actually laughed and I was glad to see it. I knew she'd come around. She put together an outfit like Madame Farsight's: a red puffy shirt; a flower-print skirt, full and down to her ankles; a gold sash around her head; gold earrings. She borrowed the skirt and earrings from her mother. "How do I look?" she asked, dancing barefoot across the room.

"Positively Bahamian."

"I think you mean Bohemian," Kathleen said.

"Yeah, that too. Help me with this cloak, would you?"

It was perfect. Long enough to drag slightly on the floor, which gave me a gliding, ghost-like quality. And I was, of course, a real ghost!

Wearing the cloak herself, Kathleen opened the front door so I could go out and then said goodbye to her parents.

"Have a good time at the party," Mr. O'Toole said.

"Isn't Casey going, too?" her mother asked.

"Yeah, she'll be along," Kathleen said. "She'll probably be the life of the party."

"Or the death of it," I whispered.

"Shh," she hissed.

We arrived a little late, as planned, to make sure everyone else would already be there. That way we could stash the cloak outside in the bushes where I could get it later. Eddie opened the door for Kathleen. He closed it so fast after her that it caught my shoe and jerked it off my heel. I stifled a scream.

"Hmm. Door doesn't seem to want to close," Eddie said, slamming it again, harder. Luckily, I pulled my foot out in time or it would have been amputated without benefit of anesthesia. But in the process I lost my shoe completely. I would have to get it later, when I returned for the cloak. "And what's that funny smell?" he said. "Must be a fire somewhere."

Eddie wore a long grey robe, a grey paste-on beard, and a pointed hat. He carried a staff. He was either a wizard, or Little Bo Peep's grandpa. "Where's Casey?" he said.

"She has something to do. It's important, she says. You know Casey."

"Yeah," he said. "I think I do." My heel ached. I wanted to knock his pointed hat right off his pointed head.

The stairs to the basement were right next to the door we came in by. That would make it easy to get the cloak. Eddie led the way down to the family room. An overhead light was on and, for some reason, a few candles were burning. Atmosphere, I guess.

Five guys were sitting around a table eating popcorn. I knew them all. Jay Randolph our right fielder, Brucie Mueller, Raymond Parker, Matt Something-or-other, and his twin, Mark Something-or-other. They look alike. Exactly alike. In fact, tonight all five of them looked alike. They were all dressed as vampires. Count Dracula #1, Count Dracula #2, Count Dracula #3 . . . What originality! What vivid imaginations!

"I'm the only girl here," Kathleen whispered.

"I'm insulted," I whispered back. A sickly smile curled the corners of her lips. Meanwhile, Brucie was spitting popcorn at Mark-or-Matt and Matt-or-Mark tilted his glass of lemonade threateningly over Brucie's head.

"Knock it off, you guys," Eddie said. "The great Kathleen the Ventriloquist" — Kathleen whispered something in Eddie's ear — "Excuse me, Kathleen the Ventriloquator is here to do her act." Catcalls and whistles from the bloodsuckers. "Proceed," Eddie said.

"I hope you can throw your voice better than you can throw a softball," Jay said, and his brothers in blood hooted.

Eddie told everybody to shut up. He suggested that Kathleen throw her voice into the lamp. That was easy. I was standing right next to it. Kathleen said, "Hi, lamp. What have you got to say?"

"Nothing much," I answered in a tiny voice. "I'm just a lamp. I sit here all day with nothing to do. Then I sit here all evening and watch TV with Eddie. Then I sit here in the dark. It's really boring."

"I come over sometimes," Jay said to the lamp.

"That's true," I said. "I prefer the dark." Kathleen winced, but everybody else laughed. Everybody but Jay. I thought he had it coming.

"Talk like Casey," Eddie said.

"Talk like Casey?" Kathleen repeated.

"Yeah, you know, like you did when you told me about the ventriloquation."

"What's ventriloquation?" said Matt-or-Mark.

"I never heard of it," said Mark-or-Matt.

"You'll see," Eddie told them.

"Okay," Kathleen said, "here goes." She sucked in a deep breath. "Hi, Casey."

"Hi, Kathleen," I said in my own voice.

"Say hi to everybody."

"Hi to everybody," I said.

"Wow! It really sounds like Casey, like she's over here by the lamp," Jay said, moving right toward it and me.

I jumped to one side, almost knocking into Mark-or-Matt. Or was it Matt-or-Mark? "Can you make it sound like she's over there?" he asked. He just missed jabbing his finger in my eye as he pointed across the room toward the stairs. I tiptoed lopsidedly across the room. With the one shoe missing it was like my legs were different lengths. Luckily the whole downstairs was carpeted.

Kathleen turned toward the door. "So what do you think of the party, Casey?"

"Hey," I said, "I thought this was supposed to be a masquerade party. Why didn't you guys wear costumes?"

"How do you do that, Kathleen?" Jay asked, ignoring my very clever jab.

"Just talent, I guess," Kathleen said. I gave her a useless dirty look.

"Can you make it sound like she's sitting in that chair?" Eddie asked, pointing to an upholstered chair in the corner. I wended my way around several vampires and sat in the chair.

"Sure, why not?" I answered smugly.

"That's really great, Kathleen," Eddie said. I noticed he was talking to Kathleen, but he was staring right at my invisible lap. I looked down. The seat cushion was depressed beneath me. Something you don't see everyday. "Casey, I hear you've got important things to do and that's why you couldn't come tonight. Wonder what they could be?" Eddie asked. All the while, he was taking little steps toward the chair, the way a cat does when it's sneaking up on a bird.

"Uh . . . I'm just doing this and that . . . you know," I stammered.

"Like what?" Another tiny step. For the life of me, I couldn't think of anything to say. And I felt a sneeze coming on. I squeezed my nose tight.

"Finding more secret rooms, maybe?" Eddie asked, edging still closer. He hadn't blinked in about a minute. I was feeling like Tweety Bird, with Sylvester just outside the bars.

I tawt I taw a puddy tat.

"Did you leave Bumps at home tonight so he wouldn't be in the way?" Eddie asked.

"Yeah, I . . . what?"

Suddenly Eddie was airborne, his arms outstretched, headed for a crash landing on the chair. I leaped out just before he would have squashed me.

I did! I did taw a puddy tat!

Eddie righted himself in the chair, sat up straight and leaned back, laying his hands on the armrests. He had the whole surface of the chair covered, like he was guarding it. "Make her say some more. From the chair again," he said.

"Okay," Kathleen agreed.

Okay? What does she mean, okay? I'm not about to jump into any chair with Eddie. I stepped on her toe. "Stop it," she said.

"Stop it?" Eddie said. "Stop what, Kathleen?"

"Stop . . . stop . . . I don't know. Stop jumping around like that, Eddie. It makes me nervous. I'm going to hold a seance now," she announced, much to my relief, "and I can't do a good seance if I'm nervous." She stood by the table. "Over here," she said.

Everyone gathered around the card table. Kathleen put one of the candles on the table and sat down. She asked everyone to join hands. Most of them didn't like that idea much and Brucie Mueller wouldn't do it at all.

"Everybody has to hold hands or it won't work," Kathleen said. "The power of the circle will be broken."

Brucie finally gave in. "Okay," he said to Mark-or-Matt and Ray, who were positioned on either side of him. "You can hold my hand. But just remember, I'm not holding yours." Then he clenched their hands like it was a wrestling match, or some kind of contest. Ray took him up on it and pretty soon the two of them were grunting and shoving each other back and forth.

"What are you two guys trying to prove?" I said. "If it's your manhood, you'd better wait a few years."

Everyone stared at Kathleen. "Just imitating Casey," she said. Nobody quit staring. She closed her eyes. "I feel a trance coming on," she said.

She took a deep breath. In Madame Farsight's trance voice she said, "I feel the presence of a poltergeist in this room." I decided to give her a hard time for the near disaster she had gotten me into at the chair. I didn't do anything. "I feel the presence of a poltergeist in this room," she said, louder. I still didn't move. "I STILL FEEL IT," Kathleen nearly shouted. "AND I'M SURE IT'S A POLTERGEIST."

Brucie snickered. I blew out the candle on the table. Brucie shut up.

"There's a breeze in here," Mark-or-Matt said.

"Yeah," said Matt-or-Mark in a voice that quavered just like his brother's. "Somebody's blowing on the candle."

I flicked the light switch off and on and off. "Yeah, somebody quit blowing on the light switch," Eddie said, looking across the table at Matt and Mark.

I grabbed a table leg and bounced it up and down. "Who's doing that?" Matt-or-Mark asked.

"Are you doing that, Kathleen?" Ray said.

"How could she?" Eddie said. "You and I have hold of both her hands."

"Maybe with her knee," said Brucie.

"Yeah, she did it with her knee," Matt and Mark chimed in unison.

"I guess that's how she did the light, too. Right, Brucie?" Eddie smirked.

I picked up the bowl of popcorn and dumped the remains on Brucie's head. Everybody laughed, except for Brucie. A second later I plunked the empty plastic bowl over Ray's head. Then I blew out all the candles except one, which I carried across the room. The vampires cowered around the seance table, their eyes glued to the candle gliding toward them. Nobody was

91

laughing anymore. The looks on their faces were worth a million bucks.

As they watched the candle hang suspended over the table, I pinched its flame out and let it drop. The darkness was total. There was a chorus of screams and curses. I felt my way to the stairs, then stumbled up to get the cloak outside. I paused a moment at the top, catching my breath and gloating over the marvelous mayhem below. A sudden burning chill invaded me. It must have been a premonition.

An instant later, a hand gripped my arm.

⇌ Fourteen ⇌

Godzilla was destroying Tokyo all over again downstairs. People yelling, furniture thumping against walls, at least one broken lamp or dish. Eddie was going to be grounded forever.

But I wasn't able to enjoy it. I was being pushed and shoved and pulled out the door. In the light of the porch lamp I saw that it was Eddie who had hold of me.

"Casey, this is you, isn't it?" he said in a voice laced equally with excitement and fear. "It better be," he muttered. He squeezed my arm really tight with one hand and with the other he reached for my head, pawing it like it was a melon in a produce bin. He looked like a madman. I twisted and turned, trying to break his grip. "It is you," he said again, in a voice still less than certain. "Come on, Casey, admit it. Only you could pull off something like this. Besides, I can tell by the smell."

"What?" I blurted.

Oh great, I thought. Now I've gone and done it. But there was one benefit. My voice startled Eddie and he loosened his grip for a second. I pulled out of his grasp, yanked off my remaining shoe, and ran down the sidewalk in my stockinged feet. Eddie didn't follow. Lucky for him, too, considering the mood he'd put me in.

I sat down to wait for Kathleen on her porch steps. What did Eddie mean, "I can tell by the smell?" I asked myself. I hope I never see him again. Maybe I'll change schools for sixth grade. Maybe I'll become Catholic and go to Kathleen's school. Join the French Foreign Legion. Go to the South Pole. Anywhere Eddie Maskit isn't.

Kathleen showed up, wearing the cloak around her shoulders and a big smile on her face. She tried to be mad at me for not waiting where we'd planned and for leaving the cloak behind but she was too pleased by her success. She told me that after the candle thing the vampires were falling all over themselves. Finally, someone found the light switch and Brucie, of all people, told her it was great and would she do it again.

"Then they started chanting 'Kath-leen! Kath-leen!'" she said. She stood up, tilted her head back and primped her hair. "They think I'm quite talented."

I'd created a monster. Or worse yet, a celebrity.

"Have you forgotten that you are only half an act?" I said. "And that without the other half you're no act at all?"

"Well, I couldn't very well give you credit, could I? We were tricking them, remember? Your idea?"

"Great. So what are you going to do to entertain at your next gig?"

"I assumed you would accompany me, of course."

"Uh-uh. This was my last appearance, or non-appearance, in public." I told her about Eddie.

After a short silence she said, "He can't prove it was you, can he?" Probably afraid this would ruin her new-found fame.

"I don't know. Of course not. But he said some strange things to me over at the lot this morning."

"At the lot?"

"Yeah. I was looking around for the trailer when he showed up out of nowhere. He said he'd see me at the party and that you wouldn't do your act unless I was there, too."

"Doesn't prove anything," she insisted.

"No, it doesn't. But it was the way he said it, as if he knew something."

We went inside. Even though she wouldn't admit it, I could tell Kathleen was a little distracted. She put her pajamas on backwards.

*   *   *

The next day dawned bright and clear. Just the opposite of the way I felt. But I was kind of glad to see that I was visible again, even though that meant my invisibility had only lasted about fifteen hours this time. Being invisible was getting too complicated.

Then Kathleen complicated everything right up again by telling me my mom had called. "She wanted to thank my parents for having you over so much lately. Luckily, they're out all day today. I promised to give them the message. Also, your mom said Bumps is missing."

Not him, too, I thought.

I ran home barefoot, carrying my socks and shoe and worrying about Bumps. Eddie was sitting on my front steps, balancing a stick on the tip of his finger. By the time I noticed him it was too late to hide.

"I was hoping you'd show up this morning," he said, concentrating on the wobbling stick.

"Why shouldn't I show up, Eddie? This is my house. I live here. Maybe it's a hard concept for you to grasp since you live under a rock."

Eddie was immune to my insult. His world consisted of his finger and a stick. Just as it was about to fall he flexed his fingertip and flicked the stick toward the cloudless sky. I watched it tumble, end over end like a miniature gymnast, until Eddie sprang off the step and snatched it out of the air two feet in front of my nose.

"Casey, this is really exciting! I mean, I had hold of an invisible person last night." I gave him my blankest look. "You, Casey! You!"

"You're crazy, Eddie," I countered. "And you're trespassing."

Eddie wasn't afraid of going to jail. "I had my suspicions before, but it was last night that I finally knew for sure." His eyes glittered.

"What suspicions?" I asked with suspicion.

"Ever since that day at the ball field. That ball I hit should have gone to the end of the lot. It should have been a homer easy. But something stopped it. And it wasn't your glove, Casey."

"Doesn't prove anything," I said, parroting Kathleen. Eddie slipped the stick into his hip pocket, like he did once in second grade with a half-used sucker I gave him.

"And the next day, when I caught up with Kathleen and you talking. You know, when she pretended to be practicing ventriloquism. I thought I heard the word 'invisible' and something about a secret room. And Bumps was there, too, and he always sticks with you, Casey. And when you said, 'Hi, Eddie,' I mean, it almost fooled me. It really did. But it was hard to believe that Kathleen could throw her voice and imitate yours *and* sneer my name the way you always do. I don't think anybody could."

He reached for the stick again, slapping it on his palm. "And then there was the rock, the one you kicked across the street." I remembered that darn rock. "Don't feel bad," he consoled enthusiastically. "It could have happened to anybody."

"Eddie, you're completely bonkers."

"And the stuff you said last night, especially that stuff with Ray and Brucie —"

"They deserved it," I said. "Every word."

"So you admit you were there."

"No, I don't. I never said that."

"You just did, Casey."

"No, I didn't. You did."

He threw the stick in exasperation. It landed in the snowball bush. "Look," he said, "I started saying about the stuff you said to Ray and Brucie, stuff Kathleen would never say in a hundred years, and you interrupted and said that they deserved it."

"I said they deserved it but I didn't say that I said it. And I never said I was there."

"Well if you weren't there then how do you know what I'm talking about? *What* did Ray and Brucie deserve?"

"First of all, it's a basic rule: Ray and Brucie deserve anything they get, as long as it's bad. Second, did it ever occur to you that Kathleen is my friend and maybe she told me everything?"

"Sure. But I don't think that's what happened."

"Well what if I told you that *is* what happened?"

"Then I'd say you were lying."

"So now you're calling me a liar."

"No, I'm not. You never said that *is* what happened."

"That *what* is what happened?"

Eddie opened his mouth. His finger was cocked and ready to wag. But he hesitated, and in that moment I could see he was lost. I let go a noisy sigh of relief.

"But what about the smell?" he said. "It was there that day I was talking to Kathleen. The same odor that's at the lot sometimes." His eyes flicked up, like he was reading from a cue card up near the guttering somewhere. "And I smelled it on you again last night."

"There you go with the smell thing again. I hate it when you say I smell."

"Again?" Eddie said. "Again? The only other time I said anything about it was last night. To the person I had hold of at the door, Casey." He had me trapped, like a mouse in a corner. "And anyway I didn't say it was a bad smell. Everybody has a smell. Believe me. I've got a fantastic nose," he said.

"You sure do," I said, making my escape right under Eddie's larger-than-average nose.

"I mean my sense of smell is fantastic. Like right now I can tell your mom is cooking oatmeal."

"How do you know?"

"Because, I can smell it," he said. He sniffed and licked his lips. "Got a little cinnamon in it."

"I don't smell anything," I protested.

"That's just my point, Casey. I do."

The smell thing was getting on my nerves. "You never told me what you smelled last night. Huh, Eddie? What smell? Cinnamon oatmeal?"

"Burning leaves," he said. "Weeds. Something like that."

He was closing in for the kill. I decided on a risky tactic. It's something in a detective's blood I guess. I had taken a shower at Kathleen's, a regular shower, after the party. I hoped any magic soap smell that might have lingered then had gone down the drain.

"And do I smell now?" I challenged.

Eddie sniffed. He leaned closer and sniffed again. Once more and he was going to have a broken sniffer.

"No," he said.

"That's right, Eddie. Now tell me, when *do* I smell, like a burning bush or whatever?" Eddie drew meaningless lines in the dirt with the edge of his shoe. "Think hard, Eddie."

"When you're invisible, I guess."

"When I'm not there, you mean. I smell when I'm not there and that proves I'm invisible. See, Eddie, *that's* crazy. You should just turn yourself in and save the crazy house people the trip."

Eddie jammed his hands in his pockets and drew some more lines. "You think you're fooling everybody, Casey. You're good with words and now you can even be invisible." He erased his art work and looked me straight in the eye. "You think you're hiding. But it's not working."

"Hiding?" My voice was shrill. "What am I hiding?"

"That you like me for one thing. And that you're nosey, just as nosey as I am, for another. You think you can hide that by being invisible. When you're invisible you can nose your way into everybody's business and they're not supposed to know, right?" I glared at him with all the glare power I could muster. "And you're mad at me because I figured it all out. Most of it, anyway. I still don't know how you actually get invisible."

"It all goes together," I said. "You think I like you. You think I smell when I'm not there. You think I'm invisible. And I think I've been wrong about you all along, Eddie Maskit. I always call you Nosey Eddie but you must be Crazy Eddie. Or maybe you're Crazy Nosey Eddie."

I marched up the porch steps like sane people do when they're tired of talking to a crazy person. I heard a rustling sound and peeked for just a split-second. Enough to see Eddie reaching into the snowball bush. Maybe he really was crazy.

"Casey." The word struck my back like a blow.

I paused on the top step, facing away from him to show my complete disdain. "What now, Crazy Eddie?"

"I believe you left this at my house." His voice was flat, self-assured. Curiosity won out over disdain. I turned.

In Crazy Nosey Eddie Maskit's hand was my missing shoe.

⇌ Fifteen ⇌

"That's not mine," I said, trying to sound casual and convincing. Not an easy task, since I was holding its mate in my hand. I backed into the house, closed and latched the door behind me. What was I going to do with only one shoe? What was I going to do with Eddie?

Things only went from bad to worse when I came into the kitchen. I lifted the lid from the saucepan on the stove. "Why did you have to make oatmeal today of all days, Mom?" I demanded.

"My! Here's someone who got out of bed on the wrong side."

"What's the brown stuff on top?"

"Cinnamon."

"Did you tell Eddie Maskit we're having oatmeal this morning? With cinnamon?"

She tilted the pan and spooned the porridge into my bowl. "Casey, you know I've been getting Eddie's approval on our menus for months now." My eyes must have bulged pretty big. "Just joking, honey. Tell you the truth, I'm not sure who Eddie Maskit is." I poured milk in a thin, careful stream. Too little and I'd choke; too much and it was soup. "Did Kathleen tell you I called?" Mom said.

Bumps! My encounter with Eddie had made me forget my reason for hurrying home.

I ate. Mom told me about Bumps. She'd let him out last night, just like usual she said, only he wasn't waiting at the door to get back in ten minutes later. They whistled and called and Dad drove around the block. Bumps still wasn't back this morning. "Maybe he's gone back to the people he lived with before he came here," she said.

"But that's been" — I counted on my fingers — "that's been over seven months. Why would he go back now?" I knew he was angry at me last night for leaving him behind, but I didn't think he would run away.

I made some **LOST DOG** signs to put on the light posts. When I went out the door I saw that Eddie had left my shoe on the step. I gave it a wide berth and set out on my search for Mr. Bumps. When I didn't find him after looking and calling for hours, I tried the animal shelter. No luck. I plopped down, discouraged, on the sidewalk and felt its heat try to burn me through my pants. I scuffed my feet in the gutter, pushing sand and bits of leaves into a small dam. Maybe Mom is right, I thought. Bumps hasn't been happy with me since the day I started being invisible. Maybe he just went back where he came from. Or maybe he thought any place was better than with me.

This was the pits. Bumps was gone. Uncle Terence was gone. My coin and the pot of gold were gone. My best friend was ready to abandon me for a career in show business. And nosey Eddie knew much, much,

much more than I wanted him to know. My life was a shambles.

My tongue found a flake of oatmeal and skillfully pried it from its hiding place between two back teeth. I thought about what Eddie had said about the smell at the lot yesterday. Maybe he does have a fantastic sense of smell. He was right about the oatmeal. So, if he smelled the burning leaves odor yesterday, then maybe the trailer *was* there, even though I didn't find it. Maybe it was invisible and had just been moved.

The thought perked me up. I would solve the mystery of Dr. Poof, Madame Farsight, Kevin, and the soap all by myself. Maybe then I would write a book about it: *Detective Casey and the Carnival Caper.* I didn't need Kathleen or Uncle Terence, and certainly not Eddie. Or even Mr. Bumps if that's the way he wanted to be about it. Although I'd miss him most of all.

By the time I got to the lot I was determined to find some answers. The trailer was there, and it was visible. Just moved back about twenty feet. That was answer number one. Unfortunately, the rest of the answers didn't come so easily. But my hunch was that everything was tied somehow to the trailer and its strange occupants.

I stood outside and looked the funny little old caravan over, feeling more confident every second that all the answers I needed were inside. I was going to get in there and find them. And I intended to do it without becoming invisible. Invisibility had gotten me into enough messes already.

I stood on the bare wooden step and knocked. The flimsy door rattled. When there was no answer, I turned the doorknob and pulled it open a bit. Nobody jumped out at me, dragged me inside, threw a sack over my head, and pushed me into a dark closet.

I stepped up and stood motionless in the doorway, my eyes and ears turned up to maximum sensitivity. The trailer seemed to be empty. For the first time, I noticed that the smell of burning leaves wasn't just on Madame Farsight or the soap. It permeated the place. Eddie Maskit could be a detective using his nose alone.

I eased down the hallway to the bedroom. No one there. I went straight to the desk and the drawer that held the documents. It was empty.

I heard a noise, right there in the room with me. Before I could panic, Bumps poked his head out from under the bed. He wagged his tail, stood up on his hind legs and fell against my thigh. "Bumps!" I exclaimed, and bent to pet him. Growls of canine excitement cascaded over me and his tongue reached for my chin. I stood up. I don't like a sticky face. Besides, I was a little hurt and angry.

"So, you've joined forces with the enemy," I said. "Or did they kidnap you, too?" He snaked back and forth between my legs, petting me with his body. "Okay. Okay, I forgive you," I said and he settled down on a rug near the door.

I went back to my search. I opened the second drawer. There it was: Kevin's birth certificate. And below it, the other papers.

There were two identical leather-covered booklets of some sort, a manila envelope crammed with full-size sheets, and a larger single sheet with gold embossing along the edges. At the top, in bold, ornate lettering were the words "Certificate of Marriage." It was for Helen Conway Voss and Paul Benjamin Spelling. Six years ago. These must be the names of Kevin's parents, I thought. But why would kidnapers steal the parents' marriage certificate, too?

I opened one of the twin booklets. It was a diploma. Not for high school, or even college. It was for a doctorate degree in biochemistry. The name on it was Paul Spelling. The other was for Helen Voss Spelling, a doctorate in Botany and Plant Chemistry. Something very strange was going on. Two carnival sideshow hands had stolen Kevin and were trying to impersonate his two highly educated parents.

A chill took hold of me and shook me like a rag doll: I hoped they weren't impersonating his two *dead* highly educated parents.

I pulled out the manila envelope, and removed the thick sheaf of papers inside. It was a contract of some sort. A lot of money had been awarded to Drs. Helen and Paul Spelling by the National Academy of Sciences to continue their research on the discovery and cataloguing of exotic plants. Attached to the last page were two laminated identification cards. The names on the cards were Helen Voss Spelling and Paul Spelling. But the faces — with different hair, not so much make-up, and minus the headgear and jewelry — looked a lot like Madame Farsight and Dr. Poof.

I sat down heavily on the desk chair. Madame Helena Farsight was Helen Conway Voss Spelling. Dr. Poof was Paul Benjamin Spelling. And they *were* Kevin's parents, just like Uncle Terence said. But then why were they posing as runaway carnival performers? There had to be more here.

Like a good detective, I pulled the top drawer out and felt under it. But nothing was there. I tried the next drawer. Nothing. Again and again, all the drawers. Nothing. I bit my lip and clenched my fists. What if the Spellings come back and find me in here? Maybe I'd better leave.

But I couldn't go. Not yet. There must be something else the Spellings were hiding. Something to explain the invisible soap or the missing gold or what had happened to Uncle Terence. I went through all the drawers again and found the same nothing. In frustration I yanked at the top one, forgetting it was empty, and it came all the way out of the desk.

And there it was, taped not to the bottom but to the back of the drawer itself. A piece of paper with writing on it. Not words. Some of the markings looked like math and others looked like hieroglyphics.

In a sudden burst of detective intuition I knew what I was looking at: the formula for the magic soap. Which meant, of course, that it wasn't real magic at all. It was an invention. Made by scientists in a laboratory. Reproducible by anybody with the right ingredients and the ability to read chemistry.

I preferred magic.

The outside door squawked and a moment later the trailer shimmied as though in an earthquake. Bumps barked ferociously and a herd of buffalo thundered in the hall. My heart lurched. I whirled around to find myself looking up at two giants in wrinkled suits. The lead giant had a head the size of a basketball and just as bald. His menacing button-eyes bore holes in me and he wagged a half-missing finger at the paper in my hand. His mouth opened and his tongue thrashed like a fish on a hook.

"I'll take that," he snarled.

⇌ Sixteen ⇌

I didn't like his attitude. Or his breath.

"Who are you?" I said. Button Eyes didn't answer, except to advance a half step and wag his stub again.

"This?" I clenched the formula a little tighter. "My homework? No way."

A bubble of saliva formed at the corner of his mouth. "Don't gimme no line, sister."

He advanced again, close enough to touch me. Bumps growled. "You shouldn't be in my room," I said. "You better get out."

"Not without the paper, kid. Just gimme the paper, that's all." His voice was as deep as his body was wide, and rasped as though sandpaper were lodged in his throat. I backed up an inch. I was practically sitting on the desk.

"If you don't get out now I'm going to have to call the police," I threatened. His beady eyes danced and his mouth softened into what looked something like a smile.

"Oh, that's very scary, sweetheart. I'm very scared. Watcha gonna call 'em with? I don't see no phone." He looked around the room, then turned his hands up in sympathy, mocking me. "I don't see no cop radio."

"Help! Help!" I yelled.

"Oh yeah, like somebody's gonna hear ya way out here."

My nose tickled. I held back a sneeze.

"Shut up, Harry." The other guy slapped Button Eyes hard on the shoulder with the back of his hand and wedged past him into the room. "You're scarin' the kid. Look, she's crying."

"I am not crying," I protested. "My eyes are watering. I've got a cold."

"I apologize for Harry here," he said. He was nearly as big as Button Eyes but his voice was silky and flowed out like a song. "You're absolutely right. We shouldn't be barging in, demanding things. But you've got to understand our situation, honey. What's your name?"

I didn't answer.

"My name's Louis," he said. "Louis Freeman." He stuck out a hand, the nails full and smooth and clean. I didn't shake it. "This is Harry. Now, I'm going to be completely straight with you. We represent Jefferson University in its efforts to recover some property that was stolen."

"Are you cops?"

Button Eyes answered. "We're the collection agency." He laughed.

Louis Freeman turned on him. "Will you shut *up*?" he said, his voice suddenly hard and brittle. "You keep scaring her. She's a little girl. We don't need for you to scare her all the time." He turned back to me. "I'm sorry," he said again. "I really am." The music had returned. "Don't mind about Harry. He's a good guy. He just doesn't know how to be with kids. Me? I've got three kids." His voice was soft. Comforting. "All girls. One just about your age. What are you, twelve?"

"Eleven," I said, and wished I hadn't.

"Eleven. That's my Annie," Louis Freeman said. "Eleven and a half, she says. 'Daddy, I'm eleven and a *half*.'" He said it in a man's imitation of a girl's voice. "She can't wait until she's a teenager. I hate to see her grow up so —"

"Why are you here?" I asked.

"Sure, that's a good question. You don't want to hear my family history, do you? Of course not." He laughed. A short laugh. He shuffled his feet and cleared his throat. "Harry and I are professors at Jefferson University. We're colleagues of the Spellings. We —"

"He doesn't look like a professor," I said, indicating his partner. Button Eyes' mouth moved but no sound came out.

"Harry's an assistant professor, actually," Louis Freeman said.

"I'm his assistant," Button Eyes said, as though this were an important clarification.

"But it's like I was saying. Your friends here," Louis Freeman gestured vaguely, as though he thought the trailer itself was my friend, "they were hired to do some work. By the University. Jeff U. You know where that is? Out in University City?" I was like a stone. "Doesn't matter. Anyway, they did the work. Good work, too. It was research. Scientific research, for the Academy of Sciences."

He seemed to know everything. Maybe he was telling the truth. Maybe I could trust him.

"The government gave them a grant. You know, money. To study plants. Find new foods, medicines. Stuff like that. But the thing is, once they did it they took off with some of the information." He pointed to the paper in my hand. "It wasn't right," he said. "They got paid. The government and the University just want what's theirs. You understand, don't you?"

I wasn't sure.

"And, of course, the University is prepared to extend a reward to you for helping out." His hand flashed inside his suit coat and emerged with a packet of bills. The top one had "100" in the corners. Louis Freeman fanned the bills. There must have been twenty of them. They were all hundreds.

He pulled at his pant legs and went down on one knee. "They're good people," he said. "Good researchers, too. They just made a mistake."

Something moved at the edge of my vision: Button Eyes, wiping sweat off his gnarled forehead.

"You're their friend," Louis Freeman said quietly. "You could help them." He reached out, in slow motion, offering me the money fan with one hand and reaching with the other toward the formula, which dangled like a wilted flower from my finger tips. "Give me the paper," he soothed. "There won't be any trouble." His voice was a whisper. His eyes held me. "It'll be good for everybody."

I felt dreamy. It made sense, what he said. His fingers inched forward. Slow. Patient. Maybe I should give him the formula.

A growl, thin and full of warning, slid from Bumps' throat. His eyes darted from one man to the other and his body quivered like a too-tight spring.

Louis Freeman heard the growl. He started, lost his balance, caught himself. His coat gaped open for a moment and I glimpsed leather and steel at his left armpit. I scrunched into the corner where the desk met the wall. "I didn't know professors carry guns," I said.

Anger flashed across Louis Freeman's smooth, round face. His eyes turned to flint. He stood up, adjusting his suit coat on the way.

Button Eyes shifted his bulk impatiently. He grabbed the bills from Louis Freeman and dropped them onto Kevin's bed. "Look," he said, "take the money or don't take the money. Either way, we're takin' what we came for." He made a grab for me and I slid along the wall to the left, barely escaping his clutches.

Bumps lunged at my assailant. His teeth found flesh. Button Eyes screamed and kicked and Bumps caromed like a pinball off his tree trunk legs. Then Bumps snatched the formula from my hand. He tore back into and somehow through that fleshy forest and into the hall.

Button Eyes stumbled into Louis Freeman. They flailed and fell, struggling like upturned turtles, shaking the little trailer like an explosion and clogging my only escape route. I grabbed a glass paper weight from the desk top and waited. But when they got back on their feet they weren't interested in me anymore. They took off after Bumps, and I took off after them.

Bumps was out the open door. The big men rumbled down the hall and out the narrow opening after him. I reached the door just in time to see Bumps disappear with the formula into the big clump of juniper bushes that runs along the right field line.

"Go, Bumps! Run!" I yelled. I heaved the paper weight at his pursuers' backs but they were too far and it landed in the grass with a harmless thump.

A long minute later Bumps emerged from the other end of the junipers, his mouth empty. Louis Freeman kicked at him but he dodged easily and ran back to me at the trailer. "Bumps, why did you leave the formula in the bushes? They're going to find it for sure." As though my words had cued them the men tore into the foliage like wild animals. They dug into the muddy earth under the bushes with their bare hands and punctuated their efforts with curses.

That's when Eddie and Kathleen came strolling down the sidewalk that runs alongside the junipers. Eddie waved to me with a big, high wave, then patted his pocket. I had barely ever seen Kathleen and Eddie together before and here they came, looking like an ad for underarm deodorant. Eddie waved again, patted his pocket again, and pointed to Kathleen. Then she pointed in the direction of her house. Eddie pulled a strip of something white part way out of his pocket, then stuffed it back and patted the pocket a third time.

I began to get the picture. "Good work, Bumps," I said.

The "professors" were still digging for treasure. I grabbed Bumps in my arms. Maybe it wasn't the logical thing — Bumps can run and dodge faster than I can. But I felt like I could protect him. They couldn't hurt him if he was with me. I wouldn't let them. "Let's get out of here," I said.

We headed around the corner of the trailer. I had an intuition that one of the thugs had seen us, but I didn't care. I had Bumps. I was strong. I was fast.

I cut through the yard behind the lot and stole a glance over my shoulder. Both men were after us. They may have been as nimble as stuffed turkeys in the confines of the trailer but it was a different story out here. Out here they were greyhounds.

I took all the short cuts to Kathleen's that I could think of: across Ms. Fithfinder's back yard, through the thin spot in the hedge, down the alley, through Old Man Ferguson's rose garden, and over the chain link fence at the back. I lost some time there because I couldn't lift Bumps over the fence and even if I could have I wouldn't want to drop him because he's not a cat. I put him down and showed him his regular place, and even though Mr. Ferguson had filled it in again, Bumps managed to scoot through.

Bumps dashed the remaining block on his own and I followed as fast as I could. My pursuers were close enough that I could hear their grunts and curses close behind when I lurched up the steps of Kathleen's porch. Suddenly the door opened wide. It was Eddie. He must have been watching for me. I stumbled through the opening after Bumps and Eddie slammed the heavy door and double locked it.

"They've got guns," I said in a voice smoldering with fear.

There was banging then, and furious yelling from the other side of the door. "Get down," Eddie whispered and dropped to all fours. "Follow me." A window shattered in the kitchen. I remembered Kathleen had said her parents would be out all day. Where are parents when you need them? I wondered. Or the police? Or the army?

We scurried like mice down the hallway, my heart pounding as though it intended to burst out of my chest. When Eddie stopped at the basement stairway door I tugged at his heel. "They'll find us down there," I said. "We'll be sitting ducks."

"No, they won't."

"They will," I insisted. He wouldn't listen and I didn't have time to argue. I was starting to crawl away when the basement door opened. A familiar black shoe stepped lightly in my path. I looked up.

"Uncle Terence."

⇌ **Seventeen** ⇋

Uncle Terence put a finger to his lips and pointed down the steps. Eddie went down, I followed, holding Bumps, and Uncle Terence brought up the rear.

No sooner had my foot touched the floor than, without a hug or a hello or a word of explanation, Uncle Terence took my hand in an iron grip and walked me straight toward the back wall. Reflexively, I tried to use the hand he held to protect myself from the impact. Uncle Terence held on. Nearly hysterical, I watched our hands and then our arms disappear into the concrete.

Then I was in the wall. For an instant everything was grey. Little rocks rushed at my face like asteroids at a spaceship. But there was no collision. No pain. Just a tingling throughout my body. The next thing I knew we were in the secret room.

I patted my face and looked at my arms and hands. Everything felt all right. Everything looked all right. Bumps seemed all right. There was no blood, no shredded clothing, no shards of bone. We weren't even dirty.

Uncle Terence went back through and I watched, spellbound, as he materialized with Eddie out of solid concrete again a few seconds later. This was a *very* good trick.

The gold was back. By its faint light I could see there were eight of us, including Bumps. Kathleen and all three Spellings sat around the perimeter of the room. Paul held the formula. He nodded at me and forced a smile. Bumps wagged his tail, jumped out of my arms and ran to Kevin. He licked his face and Kevin petted him with both hands in that rough, child way that dogs are so patient with. "Barky," Kevin said.

"Everybody quiet," Uncle Terence ordered. "They're coming down." We held our breaths.

"Damn. They're not here." It was Louis Freeman, singing a different tune. "They must have snuck out the back door."

Button Eyes said, "Maybe they're invisible." His words were followed by a surge of mayhem. Things crunched, fell, broke. He must have been swinging a club. Or maybe his arm. Kathleen looked like she was about to cry.

"Knock it off, Harry. We've wasted enough time here. Let's get back to those bushes. The mutt went in there with it and he came out without it. The kid was decoying us." Button Eyes grunted. There was one more vicious blow. Then pounding up the steps. Then quiet. We waited a long time without making a sound.

Then Kevin started talking to Bumps. Little kids and dogs must share a different language from the rest of us. About all I could get was something about a car key but Bumps thought it was very exciting. He bounced up and down and wagged his tail furiously.

Uncle Terence told us all to stay put while I checked things out. Not that we had much choice. He came back a few minutes later and announced that the house was empty. He didn't mention damage. He suggested we stay in the room for awhile anyway, just to be safe. Nobody argued.

"Who were those guys?" I asked the Spellings. "They tried to give me some lame story about being professors at your university."

"Not hardly," Helen said. "We don't know where they came from. They just showed up in the parking lot one night when we were leaving the lab. They wanted the formula. We told them we didn't have one. That was about the extent of the conversation."

"But you had it in your pocket the whole time, I'll bet."

Helen looked at Paul. "Not exactly," she said to me.

"Where was it, then? Wait. I know. On the computer. You had to sneak back in and erase the files after you copied them down, then you hid the paper just like they do in the movies. That's how I knew where to find it. I probably shouldn't have been in the trailer but it's a good thing I was, huh, because I did find it and just in time. Just before they got there. The first guy, with the little eyes, was mean right from the start but the other one talked pretty nice and even offered me money. They didn't fool me, only I didn't know what I was going to do because they were pretty big, they filled up the whole room practically, and then Bumps saved my life by biting the guy with the eyes and grabbing the formula and both of them fell down and then they were after him."

I took a big breath and plunged ahead.

"Then Eddie got the formula from Bumps and stuck it in his pocket and he and Kathleen had the nerve to walk right past those thugs with it." Eddie puffed with pride and grinned at me. I was beginning to see him in a new light. Still, I wished he wouldn't look at me. "If it hadn't been for Kathleen and Eddie sneaking it away those guys might have gotten Bumps *and* the formula. Instead, here it is, and here we all are, safe and sound," I finished exultantly.

Uncle Terence said, "I'm glad you're safe," and hugged me. Everybody smiled. Kevin giggled and clapped his hands.

Helen and Paul were sending eye messages back and forth. Paul twisted and pulled at the formula in his hand, wearing out the paper. Finally, he looked up and said, "Casey, there's something we think you should know." Another twist. The paper tore. "This isn't the formula."

I looked at the two ragged pieces of paper. "It's not?" He shook his head. "Where is it then?"

"It's not anywhere."

"You mean it's in your heads?"

"I mean there isn't any formula."

The day's adventure was shredding in my mind like the paper in Paul's restless fingers. "How could there not be a formula?" I asked.

Helen answered. "We were working on applications of rainforest plant materials. Like any competent researchers we documented everything we did. One night we came back after dinner to find that the material on one of our test slides had hardened. We hadn't expected that. I cleaned off the slide. Thirty minutes later half of my hand disappeared."

"We hadn't expected that either," Paul said. "We had a little more of the material. It had solidified, too. Instinctively, I hid it until we could find out what had happened, what was going on. The trouble is, we've never been able to duplicate it."

"We've tried, many times," Helen said, "without success. We told those men the truth that night in the parking lot."

"But they made it plain they didn't believe us," Paul continued. "We knew we were being watched. I cut the stuff up into a couple of soap-sized chunks, to disguise it better. We decided to take a leave-of-absence from the lab and go into hiding. First we tried to just blend into the city. We took jobs in restaurants, I did some janitoring at a school. But we always felt someone might see us and recognize us, give us away by accident. We always felt on the verge of being caught by those hoodlums."

"Then last fall the circus came to town," Helen said. "We hired on as Dr. Poof and Madame Farsight. We figured, who would recognize us in these get-ups?"

Quicker than a flash, she pulled her hair off. It was a wig. Soft blond hair cascaded down. Paul peeled off his bushy eyebrows and his own wig, too, revealing very little hair at all. Just a band of short blond hair, surrounding his head like a horseshoe.

"Oh my liver!" I said. "You guys look just like your pictures."

"Car key! Car key!" Kevin said emphatically. Bumps snuggled up to him.

"What's Kevin saying?" I asked. "Bumps sure likes it."

"That's another thing, Casey. Bumps is . . . our dog."

"Your dog?" I tried to keep the hurt from my voice.

"She means, he *was* our dog," Paul said. "We really only had him a little while. We named him Quark. Kevin calls him Quarky but he can't say it just right."

"But, didn't you want him?"

"It wasn't that," Helen said. "After we moved here with the trailer we experimented with the soap from time to time, trying to figure it out. Quark hated us being invisible. One day he just took off. When you came to the trailer, Casey, and said he was your dog I was just glad to see that he had found a good home. Last night he showed up by himself and today, when we were in such a panic to leave, we couldn't find him. We thought he'd gone back to your house. I can't thank you enough for saving him."

"He was hiding under Kevin's bed," I said. "We saved each other."

"What are you going to do now?" Eddie asked.

"Go somewhere else, I guess," Paul said.

"Couldn't you tell the police?" Eddie asked.

"We tried. They say they can't do anything unless we're actually attacked," Helen said.

"We didn't really want to get into the details, the invisibility and everything," Paul added. "That would just put us in a spotlight. And maybe a psychiatrist's office."

"How do you fit into all this, Uncle Terence?" I asked.

"Well now, maybe that's a story for another time," he said.

"We're just grateful for your help," Helen said to him, "or where would we be right now?"

"And we're grateful to you, too. All of you," Paul said, indicating Eddie and Kathleen and me. He scratched Bumps behind the ears. "You, too," he said.

"I still don't get it," I said. "If there isn't any formula, what was that paper, and why was it hidden in your desk?"

"It was a decoy," Paul said. "Those guys were so sure we had something that we decided to *have* something for them if they ever found us. We hid it to make it look like the real thing. We figured it would buy us some getaway time."

"Then I ruined it by keeping it from them."

"No, you treated it like the real thing, too. They'll be back digging around those bushes for a while and after we've made our getaway, they'll go through the trailer like cats looking for the catnip. They'll be busy for hours. Days, maybe."

"But they'll still be after you," I said.

Nobody disagreed.

Helen looked at Paul. "We'd better be off," she said.

"Let me go check things out one more time first," Uncle Terence said. As he started through the wall I grabbed his hand. Before he knew what happened we were together on the other side.

⇌ **Eighteen** ⇌

"What are you doing?" Uncle Terence said.

"Maybe you'll need some help," I said.

"I don't need any help. I'm making a phone call. That's not so hard."

"I thought you were going to check things out. Who are you calling?"

"The police."

"But they said the police couldn't help them."

"Because those fellows hadn't done anything to them. But when those guys get tired of digging in the bushes they're going to have another look around the trailer, don't you think?"

"Yeah, I guess so."

"Well, that's doing something. I'm just going to let the police know."

"Good idea," I said, starting up the steps behind him.

"You're staying here, Casey."

"But —"

"You want to help? Straighten up some of this mess. That would be a help." He didn't wait for an answer. He just headed up the stairs.

I looked around his work room. It was pretty much a shambles, although most things weren't damaged so much as dumped and scattered. I started collecting shoes, matching the pairs and setting them in a neat row along the bench top. I could hear Uncle Terence punching numbers on the phone. "Hello?" It sounded like he was on the kitchen extension. "I'd like to report a break-in in progress."

What if they're not there when the police show up? I worried. I righted Uncle Terence's chair. The arm rest fell off.

"There is no precise address," I heard Uncle Terence say. "It's a trailer, parked at the county-owned lot on Fleet Street." There was a pause. A pause during which I disappeared. "Yes, that's right," he said, "the lot at the intersection of Fleet and Sunrise." Another pause. "That's the one. There's a trailer there. You can't miss it."

I was still invisible. It caught me by surprise. Another blink situation of some kind. Only I wasn't really blinking. I was staying invisible. And the longer I did, the more my plan formed.

A minute later I was at the lot. In the trailer. Peering out the window into the fading evening.

Waiting.

The last thing I'd heard Uncle Terence say to the police was to hurry. That these were two dangerous-looking characters. I couldn't have agreed more. And I intended to make sure that they got caught. My plan was this: keep them at the trailer until the police arrive. I hadn't quite worked out the details.

I had remained invisible since the first moment I noticed it in Uncle Terence's shop. I hoped it would last — Louis Freeman and Button Eyes were on their way, trudging like trolls through right field toward the trailer. And me.

My nose tickled. Not now, I thought. I rubbed it and squeezed my eyes tight till the feeling went away. I crouched behind the little table in the dining area just as both men crowded through the door and marched single file down the narrow hall. Button Eyes went straight to the bedroom while Louis Freeman pulled open any door or drawer he could find in the hall and bathroom. "Ha!" Button Eyes bellowed. "She left the money. She don't know much what's important in life, does she?"

"It's counterfeit, Harry. You think I was giving her real money?"

"Oh."

It was a small trailer. A minute later both men were in the main room with me. They pulled things off of shelves. They opened books and shook them. Button Eyes yanked at the carpet and literally pulled it out from under me. I squeezed into the hallway, reassessing whether my plan was such a hot idea. I hoped the police would hurry.

"It's not here," Louis Freeman said. "Let's go."

"I ain't goin' till I find somethin'," Button Eyes answered.

"We'll find it," Louis Freeman said. "Maybe not tonight. Maybe not here. But we'll find it."

They opened the trailer door. They walked out. They headed for their car. Where were the police?

A few more steps, a few more precious seconds went by, and still no cops. They were getting away! I ran to the door, trying to think what to do. The answer came suddenly.

"AAAaaCHOOoo!" I exploded into the deepening dark. Both men stopped in mid-stride.

"What the —?" said Louis Freeman.

"Gesundheit," said Button Eyes.

"It's that kid," Louis Freeman said, spinning his buddy by the lapel of his coat. "With the cold."

I had solved one problem. They were coming back to the trailer. Fast. But now I had another one. Mom's warning rang in my ears: "That cold will be the death of you." Not if I had anything to say about it.

They were running now. Just before they got to the trailer I jumped to the ground, off to the side, where I wouldn't be trampled.

"Where is she?" Button Eyes demanded when they got inside.

"Well, she can't be very far, can she? Find her," Louis Freeman ordered, and slipped his gun from its hiding place. Very impolite, these guys.

I slammed the trailer door shut and pulled the steps about a foot and a half away from the trailer. A moment later the door burst open as though a bomb had gone off inside. Louis Freeman came out first. He fell hard and sprawled over the step. But what must have really hurt was Button Eyes landing on top of him.

They got up, groaning and cursing, and limped for their car. I wondered what to do next.

"Hey, there she is!" Louis Freeman had turned and was pointing straight at me. I looked down. I was visible! Not good timing. They turned and headed straight for me. I turned and headed straight for the junipers. It was my only chance.

In I went. In they followed. My size was an advantage. And the dark. But I needed something more. Like cops. Cops would be good.

"Where'd she go?" Button Eyes complained. "She was right in front of me. Now she's nowhere!" I made a quick check. Invisible again. Not as good as cops maybe but I would make do.

While Button Eyes and Louis Freeman entertained themselves in the junipers I sped back to the trailer. It was risky but, if the police ever did show up, it wouldn't do to have these guys assaulting junipers. I pushed the step back into place.

"Nyah nyah nyah nyah nyah nyah," I sang from the trailer door. "Nyah nyah nyah nyah nyah nyah." It worked like a charm. They came running like cats to milk.

"I hear her," Button Eyes said.

"But I don't see her," Louis Freeman answered.

These guys had very big bodies but very little brains. They went in. They searched. I hid behind the wheels under the trailer in case I went visual again. Then I watched the pretty flashing lights approaching along Sunrise Lane.

⇌ Nineteen ⇋

Back in the secret room I got a very big lecture from Uncle Terence, but I also got to break the good news to him and the Spellings.

"The best part was when the one cop recognized Button Eyes. He's done more illegal things than the officer could even remember. And then Button Eyes turned on Louis Freeman. 'I'm just the assistant,' he said. I think they're going to need a lot of lawyers."

"Thanks, Casey," Helen said.

"You don't have to leave now," I said.

"But I think we're going to. For a while. We already have time off from the lab, and our trailer's pretty much wrecked. We might just take some time to explore this amazing world and see what's next for us."

"But we won't be running now. We won't be hiding, thanks to you," Paul said.

Uncle Terence took Helen Spelling's hand on his right side and Paul's on his left. Helen carried Kevin. "*Au revoir*," Helen said, and they disappeared through the wall.

"How does he do that?" I asked Kathleen.

"He's a leprechaun," she murmured.

"I'm serious, Kathleen."

"Me, too," she said."

"Oh yeah, I'm sure. A leprechaun. And what are you? The tooth fairy?"

Her foot came to life with a slow, steady, tap. "You want the truth? The whole truth? Okay, I'll give you the whole truth."

"Thank you," I said.

"He's *part* leprechaun."

Uncle Terence returned and took Kathleen and me through the wall. I felt the familiar tingling. I learned in science class that the human body is mostly water. This must be what it's like to be mostly soda pop, I decided.

When I emerged on the other side, Kathleen's words suddenly didn't sound nearly so silly. All the pieces fit: Uncle Terence's trip to Ireland, the glowing gold, his small stature, even his shoes. I didn't know about going through walls but there had to be some explanation for that. And I had a feeling it wouldn't be a bit weirder than leprechauns. In fact, if Kathleen believed it, it almost had to be true.

After Uncle Terence brought Eddie through we all said goodbye to the Spellings. Paul shook my hand and said thanks. I turned to Helen. "What about the things you said to me in the trailer? About when you hide from others, that it's really hiding from yourself?"

"I don't know," she said slowly. "I'm mostly a scientist, I guess, but sometimes things just come to me. Does it fit?"

I remembered the stupid things Eddie had said to me. "Umm. Maybe." Maybe it does, I thought. Maybe I'm just plain nosey, like Eddie said. And being invisible couldn't hide the fact from anybody.

"Who knows? Maybe it was about Paul and me. We can't pretend to be what we're not forever. Nobody can."

She leaned over and kissed me on the cheek. "Goodbye," she said. "Goodbye, Eddie, Kathleen, Terence." She petted Bumps. "Goodbye, Quark. Maybe we'll come back someday. We have good friends here. And you're one of them."

Then Helen and Paul and Kevin walked out the door and through Kathleen's back yard. Helen scooped Kevin onto her hip. The three of them faded into the alley darkness. I stood there — we all did — looking after them, thinking private thoughts.

So when Bumps jumped to his feet, ran through the gate, and disappeared down the alley after them, there wasn't any way to stop him.

⇌ **Twenty** ⇌

Kathleen and Eddie volunteered to clean up the mess Button Eyes and Louis Freeman had left behind. I pretty much just stood there. In my mind's eye Bumps scampered down the steps, across the grass, and down the alley. It burned me like a knife. Bumps is gone. My good friend is gone. What am I going to do without him? I sniffled and choked, trying to hold my tears in.

Uncle Terence invited me to his room. He brought in a tray of cookies and apple juice and set them on a small table between us.

"Go ahead, darlin'," he said, "cry all you want."

And I did.

Finally, all my tears were gone. I turned away to wipe my face and blow my nose. When I could breathe again Uncle Terence pushed several of the cookies toward me and one of the glasses. He had some, too. He didn't pull out his flask of whiskey like usual.

We didn't talk. We just munched cookies and sipped juice for what seemed a long time. Two suitcases stood by the open closet door. One of them seemed to be glowing.

Uncle Terence's eyes sparkled. "I'm going on a trip," he said, answering my question before I asked.

"I thought you *had* gone on a trip."

"Well, darlin', I almost did. You see, I'd spotted those characters hanging around so I packed my bags and went to warn the Spellings and tell them I thought it was time to move again. I was prepared to go with them for awhile. But things came to a head faster than we anticipated."

"How do you know the Spellings?" I asked.

"Oh, I've known Helen and Paul a long time."

"Oh, yeah, you used to work at the university."

"That's right. I cleaned their lab every night. When they worked late we would enjoy a cup of tea together. We were friends. And that night, the night the magic soap came to be, I was there. When they needed to go into hiding I told them about the circus, where they might disappear, so to speak." He smiled at his joke. "But they're safe now, and it's time for me to do something I should have done a long time ago."

"The gold," I said, my eye on the suitcase. "The millstone around your neck."

"Yes," he said. "Except for today. Today it saved us. Without it I couldn't have gotten you and the others through that wall."

"Something to do with the gold gets you through the wall?"

Uncle Terence nodded. "That's correct. Nothing can keep a leprechaun from his gold."

"Then you are a leprechaun, just like Kathleen said."

"Only part leprechaun, actually."

"She said that, too. And your trip. That has to do with the gold and being part leprechaun?"

"Correct again. I'm taking the gold back home."

132

"Ireland?"

He nodded.

"Are you coming back?" I asked.

"Oh, yes. I've got work to do."

"What work?"

"Why shoes, of course. Making and repairing shoes. I'm good at it. It's what I've always done. More important, it's what I love to do."

"Is it your dream, like we talked about the other night?"

"It is, Casey, my girl. Recognizing your dream and bringing it into the light of day is what's important. And you can't do that if you're hiding who you really are."

"Are you a tortoise, too?"

"Not anymore," he said.

"But what about the gold? Why take it to Ireland? You said there wasn't anyone there to give it to."

He stroked his pointy ears. "You've probably noticed that my gold is a bit unusual. That's because it's fairy gold. If I were to pass it on it must go to someone with the trait. But fairy folk are few, and hard to find nowadays. All this time I thought that the proper home for the gold was with another leprechaun. But now I know a better home."

"Where?" I asked. "And why not with a leprechaun?"

"When a leprechaun has the gold, all the power is his and his alone. But when the gold is returned to Mother Earth — where it came from to begin with — the magic is passed on to the whole world." He patted the suitcase like it was a friend. "I'm going to plant this gold beneath a rainbow. It'll grow some magic, the kind that helps people see their dreams and helps them make those dreams come true. Then back I'll come to make my own come true."

He reached into his pocket. "This is something you've been missing, I believe." He held out a gold coin. My gold coin.

I hesitated. "Shouldn't that one go back, too, with the others?"

He took my hand and put the coin in my palm and closed my fingers over it. The gold throbbed quietly and sent its warmth through me. "This one's yours."

"But how did you get it? I put it under my pillow."

"Well, Casey, my dear, it's like I said, nothing can keep a leprechaun from his gold."

* * *

Kathleen and Eddie walked me home. I was glad for the company. I'd never seen Kathleen so messy. Her hair was sticking out all around and her shirt was hanging half out of her shorts. For Kathleen that was major messiness.

I told her I was sorry she was upset about Uncle Terence being a leprechaun. She said she thought she would get used to it. I figured she was right. After all, she'd gotten used to me being The Invisible Kid. I thanked her for getting mixed up in the whole adventure. She said it was Eddie's idea to track me down this afternoon. He thought I might need some help. I thanked him, too. He grinned like an idiot.

134

Shuffling up the walk to my house I felt tired. So tired. I thought I heard Bumps' familiar yip welcoming me home. And I even imagined I saw him, like a mirage, sitting on the porch. I shook my head to clear it, but only tears came. It *was* Bumps. He sprang down the steps and wiggled between my legs.

"Bumps, did you come back to stay?" He wagged his tail and smiled and licked me on the nose.

I didn't even care.

* * *

A few weeks later Kathleen and Eddie and I took the bus into the city. A cloudburst turned the streets into temporary rivers, and passed over by the time we got off. We hiked a half block through mist hissing off the steaming concrete.

When we got there I put my face to the window. Uncle Terence was hunched over his work, whistling. Kathleen and Eddie went inside. He looked up from his work and smiled. Kathleen hugged his shoulders and kissed his pointy ear.

I stepped back to get a good look. The building didn't look like anything special. But it was. The sign over the shop was painted in many colors, and shaped like a rainbow. *The Lucky Leprechaun Shoe Shop*, it said. And underneath, in bold black letters, **Terence O'Toole, Proprietor**.

Behind the shop a real rainbow splashed across the sky. I knew there was a pot of gold at the end of it.

ABOUT THE AUTHORS

Terry and Wayne Baltz were born and raised in St. Louis, although at the time they were better known as Terry Swekosky and Wayne Baltz. They now live in Colorado, where they divide their time between living in the city (with the luxuries of theaters and stores) and living in the mountains (with the luxuries of far views, deer and elk, bunnies, mountain bluebirds, eagles, and incredibly starry nights).

The authors regularly visit elementary and middle schools where they talk with children about writing, creative expression, and the publishing process. You may contact them at the publisher's address or by telephone (970/493-6593) for further information.